Herbert A. Smith

Stellar Songs and Lyrics

Herbert A. Smith

Stellar Songs and Lyrics

ISBN/EAN: 9783744767330

Printed in Europe, USA, Canada, Australia, Japan

Cover: Foto ©Andreas Hilbeck / pixelio.de

More available books at **www.hansebooks.com**

STELLAR SONGS

AND OTHER POEMS.

Ballantyne Press
BALLANTYNE, HANSON AND CO.
EDINBURGH AND LONDON

Stellar Songs

AND OTHER POEMS.

WITH AN INTRODUCTORY ESSAY ON SCIENCE AND POETRY.

BY

HERBERT A. SMITH, MD.

MEMBER OF THE ROYAL COLLEGE OF SURGEONS, ENGLAND; LICENTIATE
OF THE ROYAL COLLEGE OF PHYSICIANS, EDIN.; LICENTIATE
OF THE APOTHECARIES' SOCIETY, LOND.
AUTHOR OF "DARWIN AND HIS WORKS: A STUDY;"
"ESSAYS ON SCHOOL HYGIENE," "FUGITIVE POEMS," ETC.

Who'd grasp the stately laws, adjusting worlds
  Mighty in magnitude, must learn the play
Of atoms cast adrift—the meteor 'tis unfurls
  The secrets of the cosmos, leads the way
To the mind's grip of planets small and grand;
He stellar problems then can understand.
Stellar Songs, p. 55.

With Illustrations.

LONDON:

REEVES AND TURNER, 196 STRAND.

1891.

I DEDICATE

𝕿𝖍𝖊𝖘𝖊 𝕻𝖔𝖊𝖒𝖘

to

My old Friend and Fellow-Student,

THOMAS   FREDERICK   PEARSE,

M.D., F.R.C.S., ENGLAND; M.R.C.P., LONDON,

*A Man of Letters and a Master of his Art, whose original genius
and whose wide culture distinguish him as a man among
men, and whose many acts of kindness towards
me in the past entitle him to a lasting
place in my memory.*

H. A. S.

CONTENTS.

b

PART III.

𝕸iscellaneous 𝕻oems.

INTRODUCTORY.

ON THE RELATIONS BETWEEN SCIENCE AND POETRY.

(AN ESSAY.)

SOMETHING in the nature of an *apologia* is probably expected, and therefore shall be forthcoming from me, for producing a scientific subject in a poetic garb, for contravening the canons of an art apparently wide as the poles from the province of science. I deem it therefore fitting to adduce examples from poets who have anticipated me in this connection. Before doing so, I hold it pertinent to give a slight sketch of the universe as it is, and as it has been, affected by that law which is known as the Law of Evolution.

To the writer no subject in the whole range of thought, either in Literature, Science, or Art, bristles with such interest, has so many issues, and engages the reader's enthusiasm as that of Evolution; for it is a byword in the pulpit, it pervades the air of the class-room, and is an accepted theme in the fashionable salon—in a word, it is the prevailing thought; and for this reason, that

A

all the great discoveries of science, and revolutions in thought—the advanced speculations of Mr. Croll; the subtle investigations of Sir H. Roscoe, Professor Koch, and Sir Wm. Thompson; the telluric researches of Professor Geikie—whatever is novel in astronomy, medicine, or geology, all have alone been come to by inquiry on lines laid down in the philosophy of Mr. Herbert Spencer.

In the following study—"Stellar Songs"—it has been the author's aim to describe in verse rather than in prose the part that meteors play in space in evolving the universe; to present in an attractive guise some of the principal laws that govern the origin, life-history, and destiny of suns, planets, and stars. He has selected the unit of space—the meteor—because of its preponderance without, and because it is the body most instrumental in building up the varied orbs we see around us, because the atom has played the largest part in unfolding the solar system from a primeval state of nebular haze. Now it is not too much to say that the earth journeys through space—through swarms of meteors—pretty much as man walks through a snowstorm—hence their importance. According to Professor H. A. Newton, the average number of meteorites that the earth traverses in each volume equal to that of the earth, is about 30,000. Again, as Mr. Lockyer points out, there is from time to time discovered a new star, associated or not with nebulæ: now he considers such constellation due to the swarming of meteors. Thus we see their import.

But to proceed. It is supposed that after the evolution of the planets known to men, matter faltered awhile, and meteors fell into space pell-mell, as a residue of the complex process undergone in cooling down and building up the hosts of heaven; and that our friends, the meteors, were left pretty much as mortar remains—as the residue of the structures built up. It is thus that we begin to realise the import of the atom. But in order to understand the law of Evolution, that law of space Gravitation, has to be studied; for just as the one is a law of sustentation, so is the other an equally divine method of government, and therefore both are discussed in these pages. But to the history of Evolution. After the time of the Roman poet Lucretius, who laid the foundation of the great edifice, men's minds slept for many generations, and human progress was under a cloud. This state of things went on till the times of Galileo and Copernicus, till the time of Kepler and Newton, till the time of D'Alembert and Diderot; these were the men who raised the raw material into the stately edifice of Evolution, until it acquired the grace, harmony, and beauty imparted to it by Mr. Herbert Spencer.

So long ago as B.C. 52, Lucretius taught that the universe came into existence by collision of atoms, that these atoms fell like flakes of snow, and that some, as they bounded off from one another, caused air and sunlight, and others stone and iron; that such collisions went to make each world, which rolling, soon acquired a rhythm of its own. Now this rhythm of motion is still a law of matter. He was also right in allowing a long period for the process undergone. Here are his words :—

" Thus from the depths of all eternity
    The unwearying atoms wage a dubious war;
And now with surging life doth victory lie,
    And now anon is death the conqueror.
Such is the nature, then, of empty space—
    The void above, beneath us, and around—
That not the thunderbolt, with pauseless pace,
    Hurtling for ever through the unplumbed profound
Of time, would find an echo to its race.
    For blindly, blindly, and without design
Did these first atoms their first meetings try.

.   .   .   .   .   .

They clashed through the void space tempestuously,
Until at last that certain whirl began,
Which slowly formed the heaven and earth and man."
                            —MALLOCK.

It is thus clear that Lucretius early rocked the cradle of Evolution, but the fractious infant was not duly weaned till the time of Kant and Laplace, the latter of whom formulated what is now known as the nebular hypothesis.

Now this theory deals with the state of things before the dawn of order, and, as in the minds of *savants* there gathers such a halo of enthusiasm around this mystic process, I deem it fitting to describe briefly the hypothesis in question. Putting aside that imaginary world of fanciful atoms, fortuitously turning out of chaos an orderly universe, as set forth by Lucretius, Laplace advances the theory that in the beginning all the worlds existed *potentially* in a haze of fluid light—a nebula so vast and of such thinness as to extend to the farthest limits of space, to everywhere. Grant Allen puts it facetiously when he says "that the world arose out of a primitive world-gruel." But to pass on, this matter of which it was composed was a very thin gas—so thin that millions of cubic miles might be compressed into a nutshell. Now, slowly setting around common centres, this gas or nebula collected into suns and stars, whose light and heat is still, and has always been, due to the clashing together of the myriads of atoms as they fall towards a central mass. According to this fashionable theory, which promises to be true, the universe began as a vast ocean of nebular haze, until it became, by chemic action, changed, to use the immortal words of Mr. Spencer, "from the homogeneous to the heterogeneous, from the coherent to the incoherent, from the indefinite to the definite condition." But what is this chemic action? It is, that every star that glads the face of man is continually gathering in the hem (as it were) of its own glorious garment—is for ever growing denser and denser, till, worn out, it sets around its centre of gravity. But to render this still clearer. The all-pervading haze, as it condensed and grew less from without towards a centre, revolved rapidly on its mighty axis. The solar mist irregularly threw off concentric rings of cloud-like matter from its equator ; these rings, compressed from without, collapsed, and the fragments still revolving, underwent aggregation. Having now an orbit of their own, each mass thus aggregated formed a planet, the planets first formed being Neptune, Uranus, Saturn, and so on—always the outermost ones being the first formed. But chemic action did not stop here, for the mass first thrown off from the central core being in a molten state, and the repulsive force of its motion being greater than that of gravity, now formed another ring, and in turn detached itself from its core—in short, a satellite or moon became evolved. In some instances, *e.g.*, Saturn, as many as eight rings were in turn cast off, and these became satellites. Now, one of the most conclusive pieces of evidence that the nebular hypothesis is true, is adduced from the fact of a belt still revolving around Saturn's central mass, although disconnected from it. But we have not done with the theory, for during the settling down of the nebular haze, the main central core of all—ever retreating and condensing, in spite of parting with belt after belt—went to form the sun itself.

It is evident that this complicated and protracted process must have taken an enormous length of time to settle down into the orderly state we now know the solar system to present, and nothing short of a hundred millions of years is given by physicists. It is equally manifest, then, that the sun, stars, and planets were not manufactured straight off as for a celestial orrery, but were due to the slow, gradual, but certain working of natural laws, which laws determined their place, orbit, weight, and motion. And these facts are so irrefutable, that it is not surprising to find them gradually incorporated into the common sense of to-day, for all must in time accept them :—

> " The age will come when all will have to bow
>   To the ' Time Ruler,' spite of bitterness ;
>   The law which shows how planets grow, and how
>   They're growing still—the greater and the less :
>   ' Magic creation ' will be laid aside,
>   And faith in Evolution have full tide."
>
> —*Stellar Songs*, p. 88.

Thus the meteor becomes the unit in the growing of the heavenly bodies, just as the slender nerve-trace in a jelly-fish is the starting-point from which mind is built up in man; both are explained and made plain by Evolution. And the subject is so full of thought, so far-reaching, so philosophical, in a word, so fascinating, that it is not surprising to find it a basis of reflection in most of the great works of a scientific and oft of a literary character. With but a slight insight into its principles, it certainly appeals to every broad-thinking man, and the thought immediately arises, "Surely I must remodel my great work, be it poetry or prose, a 'Lux Mundi,' a tractate on Truth, or a manual on Theology, on the lines so eloquently advanced by Mr. H. Spencer." Yes! The noisy child pleads again and again, and commands us to adopt it; for it is a child of Nature, ever unfolding new-sense pictures of the outer world, a law of Time which is the handmaid of change, a law to which we are all born; nothing escapes it, progress is its path, and all man's greatest discoveries are but the sub-laws of its working. Then again, Evolution is a religion in itself; for the man who follows it is humble in the presence of Nature, for she is the last phase of the First Great Cause: "Some may scoff at her, the child of their god, but the Evolutionist loves her, for she is his companion, his mother, and his nurse; she ministers to his pleasure, yet ever works for his advancement: awake, he studies her, for she is the mine of his learning; asleep, he dreams of the unseen working of her wondrous laws" (Ridsdale). Man listens and as ever sees and wonders that a time should have ever been when—

" There was nothing at all,
But a motion most comic of dust motes atomic, a chaos of decimal
  fractions,
Of which each under Fate was impelled to his mate by love, or the
  law of Attractions,
So jarred the old world in blind particles hurled, and love was the
  first to attune it ;
Of the worlds thus begun, the first was the sun, who wishing to
  round off his girth,
Began to perspire with great circles of fire, and this was the cause of
  the earth."
  —COURTHOPE: *The Paradise of Birds.*

But to leave Mr. Courthope's burlesque on the great
principle, and to return to the philosophy in view. The
doctrine of Evolution is then nothing short of an ency-
clopædia on development, a very " synthesis " of wisdom,
for it embraces the world of mind and matter ; and such
a theory must gain attention, because it is a key to the
growth and order of the cosmos. It embraces growth
and decay, life and death (Evolution and Dissolution).

Nothing is omitted from the system, for it traces the
process of change through all things—through suns and
worlds, through animals and plants, mind and feelings,
organisations and societies, languages, religion, literature,
science, art, and morals. On the surface of the earth
Mr. Spencer sees unfolded continents and oceans, lakes
and rivers, rocks and strata—the whole most deftly
carved out by the great artist Nature. In animal and
plant life he sees a gradual building up of every creature
from the simple and earliest organisms, and this by two
processes—" the action of the environment " and the
" survival of the fittest." The works of Ball, Proctor,
Lubbock, Geikie, Darwin, Romanes, Max Müller, Vines,

Croll, and Sedgwick (all of which I have consulted) would possess but little value without a previous digest of Mr. Spencer's principles. The magic power with which he unfolds the secrets of the cosmos is truly enchanting; for his system embraces not only organic and inorganic growth, but surveys the realm of mind, and the vast empyrean of stars. He wanders from the growth of a crystal to that of a world, from the nature of a microbe to the genius of Mr. Gladstone, from the " bah-bah " of a savage to the mental thought required to apply the differential calculus. There would appear to be no fact in the abstract or concrete world, and no theory, with which Mr. Spencer is not familiar—such is his range of inquiry. No boundary line can, I say, be traced to his thoughts (unless it be poetry), no space or time to which his genius has not travelled.

But to the relations between Science and Poetry. Now the poetry of the sky is surely not lost because the latter is reduced to a law of physics, any more than physical phenomena—say the rainbow, the stars—lose their beauty and allegory through being reduced by Newton to elementary proportions; and a knowledge of astronomical states—even on evolutional lines—can best enlarge the boundary of our imagination. To attempt to divorce the realm of imagination from that of reason, then, can only be compared to severing the ties of mind and heart; for is not imagination the bride of reason, who appeals to man's emotional life, who sustains his heart, who sings to him sweet songs, who worships his better nature, and through whom he alone worships all that is high, lofty, and noble. This is my plea for dealing with a subject,

"Stellar Songs," that some may consider unfitted for poetical rendering. The age is essentially unromantic and prosaic 'tis true, and men's minds are more easily riveted with objective than with subjective impressions; but this is the reason why man needs, in my opinion, the poet, and why scientific forms are not injured by poetical treatment, any more than that sculpture lacks artistic proportions through a knowledge of anatomy.

No one will admit that the inventive element is endangered by a knowledge of science, for the scientific method is at first "synthetic," *i.e.*, man builds up his finished fabric from the data he has at hand, while the poet is more selective in scattering his gems—he leaves out unnecessary detail. But many so-called scientific subjects are largely in part creations of the imagination, based, it is true, on facts, and so theories: this applies to medicine, geology, and astronomy, &c. We have to do with concrete things, but interpret them from a constructive point of view: this is the case with the "nebular hypothesis," the "snow age," and the "origin of species." As Professor Thomas says—"Poetry and science have so far gone hand in hand, and have played parts of equal prominence and value in history; so it will always be, for both have their roots deep down in human instincts that are imperishable." I know that there are many who prefer a common rendering of common things, and are content with the form, colour, and imagery suggested by nature, rather than with the fuller meaning that a scientific imagination can endow them with—content with directing their hearts and minds heavenwards, with claiming fellowship with Peter Bell, of whom 'tis said—

" In vain through every changeful year
  Did Nature lead him as before,
A primrose by a river's brim
A yellow primrose was to him,
  And it was nothing more."—WORDSWORTH.

But a fuller knowledge of men and things lends the
imagination greater power of interpretation—lifts, as it
were, the mind into grander and higher thought. It is
for this reason that the trained scientific man can appre-
ciate Browning, who is the poet of a pure and exact age.
In him reason and imagination seem mated in a pre-
eminent degree, for all his creations bristle at given
periods with fiery thought and brilliant conceptions; in
him we find each flight of fancy coloured with intellectual glitter, every fact adorned with the glamour of his
art. To many, it is true, Browning is grotesque, prosaic,
and unintelligible; but that is because he is so much
wiser than they, because he has succeeded in getting at
the soul of things, while they have been groping in the
dark. To Browning, Evolution is as much a toy as a
lover's song, for does he not tell us on spectral light :—

" Only the prism's obstruction shows aright
  The secret of a sunbeam, breaks its light
Into the jewelled bow from blankest white ;
  So may a glory from defect arise."
                                   —*Poems*, vol. vi. p. 151.

Again, are we not taken into the very transept of the
temple of Evolution when we read of the inward struggles
of Paracelsus, of how " that searching and impetuous
soul" did commune with nature as to what is God, what
is life? The restless heaving throes of a changing world,

in which Evolution is still going on, were apparent to him, or we should ne'er have seen—

> " The wroth sea-waves are edged
> With foam, white as the bitten lip of hate : strange groups
> Of young volcanoes come up, cyclops-like
> Flaring together with their eyes on flame."

Browning would never have marched past the stately panorama of vital processes, and stamped his approval of the great doctrine in such words as—

> " So far the seal
> Is set on life, one stage of being complete,
> One scheme wound up : and from the grand result
> A supplementary reflux of light
> Illustrates all the inferior grades, explains
> Each back step in the circle."

In the company of the great master the beauties of nature as well as the defects fall into place like the shifting prisms of the kaleidoscope : so full of colour are they, that his range of imagery extends from science to art, from art to music, from music to religion, and from religion back again to science. One hears and sees as from an acropolis the judgment on a Prometheus unbound, as well as the secret that unfolds the flowers in spring. With him one sees, while sailing in Venetian gondolas, visions of architectural beauty and dreams of passion and crime ; you hide in archæological aqueducts, once the pride of a Roman city, and pass from the pleasures of the Arno to the miseries of the Morgue, from the tents of Shem to the wicked plains of Babylon. The struggles in the development of a soul are delineated

with the same care as are those of the body : nothing in
the whole drama of life escapes Browning, for in reading
him you travel with the patriot, who dies the death of a
martyr, to the laboratory of the chemist, who wastes his
time on the origin of life : you pass from the glittering
saloon of the pompous duchess to the saloon, I say, that
is crowded with the spoils of Renaissance art, and where
the " Bishop orders his tomb at St. Praxeds."   He forecasts the ultimate perfection of the body as well as of
the soul, for—

> " In man's self arise
> August anticipations, symbols, types,
> Of a dim splendour ever on before
> In that eternal circle run by life."

Browning can juggle as artfully in poetry with the
latest scientific theory as he can sing of the human
passions, can as fearlessly dissect the thought surrounding man's descent as he can paint the features of a
Pompilia, and for this reason—

> " That he at least believed in soul,
> Was very sure of God."—*La Saisiaz.*

The thought of his lowly origin disturbs him not, he
alone sees the goal of steady progress—that haven of
mind where Truth is enshrined, and so he cheerfully goes
on, and says—

> " I like the thought he should have lodged me once
> I' the hole, the cave, the hut, the tenement,
> The mansion and the palace ; made me learn
> The feel o' the first, before I felt myself
> Loftier i' the last."—PRINCE II. SCHWANGAN.

Browning reflects, and none knows better, that

" God takes time."

All the while—as the shuttle flies across the weaver's path, so Evolution runs through the corridors of his thoughts. Do we not see a hint of gravitation in Sordello?—

" A soul above his soul,
Power to uplift his power—this moon's control
Over the sea-depths."—Page 187.

It is only when science is the watchword of progress that anything like rich poetry obtains : in a rude age bursts of passion may fill the air, but no gems of thought encased in the feelings of the soul are struck. And that is why I linger on Browning as on a master of his art, because he makes the music of the heart complementary to that of the intellect, which is the realm of science— because in his studies he can descend from a high peak of intellectual soaring to a sequestered rose-bed of rich emotion. The dry hard facts of everyday life are seen to be capable of attraction under his care, and the domain of poetry to become enriched by his skilful handling.

Treating of the problem of life, of good and evil, beauty and deformity in " La Saisiaz," the strange beginnings of things does not escape him any more than does the nebular hypothesis—

" What though fancy scarce may grapple with the complex and immense
—His own world for every mortal ? Postulate omnipotence !
Limit power, and simple grows the complex ; shrunk to atom-size
That which loomed immense to fancy low before my reason lies,
I survey it and pronounce it, work like other work : success
Here and there the workman's glory, here and there his shame
no less !"—Page 169.

Such is Browning's commune with the mystery of the universe, but the reader must follow him further, till the "harsh throes" of imagery die off into the swell of reason's satisfaction, till the roughness of the dusky and rock-lined chamber of reflection leads to the smooth path on the cliff-where the meridian glory of hope glads the heart.

But others have echoed their scientific knowledge in verse, have invested the operations of natural laws with the enchantment of their art; and notably, Tennyson, who allows his thoughts to linger along the paths of science. In describing the witch employed by Lucilia, who poisons the philtre that is to lead Lucretius home to her love, he says—

> " For the wicked broth
> Confused the chemic labour of the blood,
> And, tickling the brute brain within the man's,
> Made havoc among those tender cells, and check'd
> His power to shape."

And then Lucretius fitfully dreams that—

> " A void was made in nature; all her bonds
> Crack'd, and I saw the flaring atom-streams
> And torrents of her myriad universe,
> Running along the illimitable inane
> Fly on to clash together again."—LUCRETIUS.

We here have the essence of the atomic theory, and something more than a hint of Evolution; for are not atoms the foundation-stones of the world, building up its parts? We have only to imagine the mortar that holds these atoms together removed, and we see the consequence—the loss of gravitation, cohesion, and affinity;

but restore nature's forces, and these "flaring atoms" tumble along through space, and then "clash together again."

Astronomy to this master-mind is no alien, no out-cast, for as Tennyson soars, does he not tell us the nature of a sun-flower as aptly and as tersely as the stately roll of "The Little Bear"?—

> " Unloved, the sun-flower, shining fair,
>   Ray round with flames her disk of seed ;
>   And many a rose-carnation feed
> With summer spice the humming air.
>
> " Unloved, by many a sandy bar,
>   The brook shall babble down the plain
>   At noon, or when the lesser wain
> Is twisting round the polar star."
>
> *—In Memoriam*, pt. 101.

He carries his verse into every camp, it may be in a less learned manner, but with more regard to detail than his great compeer, Browning. We have only to turn to "The Talking Oak" to hear him speaking like a botanist :—

> " Flower in the crannied wall,
>   I pluck you out of the crannies ;—
>   Hold you here, root and all in my hand—
>   Little flower ! but if I could understand
>   What you are, root and all, and all in all !
>   I should know what God and man is !"—Ver. 123.

Little escapes even Tennyson ! He is a man who longs to wake up a century hence to realise the secrets of the stars, to know what the disciples of Lockyer,

Roberts, and Croll have to say even on spectrum analysis. He yearns for even his Easter Day, . . . to rise—

> " And learn the world, and sleep again,
>   To sleep through terms of mighty wars,
>   And wake on Science, grown to more
>   On secrets of the brain—the stars."

Again, he shows no better example of the relations between two apparently diverse subjects, science and poetry, than in "Two Voices":—

> " To-day I saw the dragon-fly
>   Come from the walls where he did lie,
>   An inner impulse rent the veil
>   Of his old husk : from head to tail
>   Came out clear plates of sapphire mail ;
>   He dried his wings—like gauze they grew,
>   Through crofts and pastures wet with dew,
>   A living flash of light he flew."

But we must wander along the summer mead, which is rich in colour and perfume, where the busy hum of insects and the murmur of the purling stream break the stillness of the air, to realise all this, never allowing our faculties to become blunted ; we must pry into nature's secrets, and cull the lessons which they teach : be it to the sea-side, go where we may, we shall learn something—

> " Learn of the little nautilus to sail,
>   Spread the thin oar, and catch the driving gale."
>
>   —POPE.

How many poets have sung of the mood of the ocean, of its security, its temptation, and of its anger?

The poetry surrounding the combustion of a piece of

B

coal I have reverted to in "Stellar Songs" under the
resources of the sun; and surely there is beauty in the
process of the carbonic acid being split up by the sunbeam into carbon and oxygen! for may not the small
atoms of carbon go in raindrops to the ocean, or be
utilised in the growth of the elm? Whether or not we
understand the rainbow to be due to the unequal re-
frangibility of elementary rays, we no less enjoy the
interpretation of the poet, be he Milton or Byron—Milton,
as in the "Comus," or more happily Byron, as in the
"Bride of Abydos"—

> " Be thou the rainbow to the storm of life !
>   The evening beam that smiles the cloud away,
>   And tints to-morrow with prophetic ray !"

We see that the idea is an augury of hope, that a scientific
fact underlies a conception, that thought and fancy
enrich the passage, and we go away content.

Any one who has read "Paradise Lost" must have
noted the prolonged train of thought that Milton exerted
on the Ptolemaic system of the heavens. Turn to this
passage :—

> " Whether the sun, predominant in heaven,
>   Rise on the earth, or earth rise on the sun,
>   He from the east his flaming road begin,
>   Or she from west her silent course advance
>   With inoffensive pace that spinning sleeps
>   On her soft axle !——
>   Solicit not thy thoughts with matters hid,
>   Leave them to God alone !"

How many have dilated on "the stars that fought
against Sisera"?

There is poetry in the changes that even the earth undergoes; for if we walk along the sea-coast at certain places, notably Cromer, we see tree-remains where the sea now holds complete sway. Such a fact comes home! But the statement that a chalky ocean-bed underlies the Green Park in London, which re-echoes the high-toned rumble of the Piccadilly traffic, seems incredible; yet in Tennyson this scientific fact is caught up :—

> " O earth! what changes hast thou seen
> There—where the long street roars hath been
> The stillness of the central sea."

Here our author as much delights to discourse on the petrifactions of the beach as elsewhere on the arrow seeds of the dandelion: so we see poetry and science to be the twin-offspring of the same mind; we find his pen limning creations, drawn as much from reason as from imagination, from the treasury-house of thought as well as from the theatre of fancy, but then—

> " The poet's eye, in a fine frenzy rolling,
> *Doth* glance from earth to heaven, from heaven to earth,
> As imagination bodies forth the forms of things unknown."

Such is the great epic writer's soliloquy! such, in fine, the speech of Raphael to Adam!—showing the author's conjecture about the stars. Here is a poet who forecasts a time when men will presume to—

> . . . " Gird the sphere
> With centric and eccentric scribbled o'er,
> Cycle and epicycle, orb in orb."—Book viii., line 160.

He neither blames man for asking, searching, or for

questioning; great lover of truth! it mattered not to him whether—

> "Heaven move or earth
> Imports not, if we reckon right."—*Book* viii.

He saw the wonder, the beauty, and the order of things; he computed their magnitude :—

> "This earth, a spot, a grain,
> An atom, with the firmament compared,
> And all her numbered stars that seem to roll
> Spaces incomprehensible."—*Ibid.*, line 17.

What he did not understand he left, determining that—

> "The great Architect
> Did wisely to conceal, and not divulge
> His secrets, to be scanned by them who ought
> Rather admire."—*Ibid.*

But we must remember that the close of the sixteenth century was an age in which inquiry and scientific research were "under a cloud!"

With such examples, culled from heroes illustrious in the annals of poetry, bearing on abstruse and highly technical subjects of a scientific nature—examples, I say, that harmonise the higher sentiments of the heart and mind, ample excuse is mine for writing on a formal and prosaic subject. But what theme awakens our enthusiasm like that of the heavens—the laws of space? The mysteries of the empyrean and the physics of the sky are surely as attractive as that allegory of the sky that—

> "Gives to airy nothings
> A local habitation and a name!"

With Wordsworth and Buchanan I have always pos-

sessed boon companions, and whiled away many an hour
in the fields of pastoral poetry : these are the men who
afford recreation to the mind and heart, for both commune on nature, although on lines of simplicity more
pronounced than their great compeer Tennyson, or even
Browning. In the still, soft, dreamy days of leafy June,
I hesitate not to say that I would rather travel with the
former than the latter. Now, these poets enchant but never
tire ; they invariably satisfy the heart, but the mind never
stands a chance of banqueting. As a poet on natural history—on men, women, and things ; on the habits, haunts,
and characters of the creatures of fur and feather ; of all
living things that breathe and move, even to the green
grass—few men have appealed to my sympathies more than
Robert Buchanan. Who would not linger with him when—

> " There is a singing in the summer air,
>   The blue and brown moths flutter o'er the grass,
>   The stubble-bird is creaking in the wheat,
>   And perched upon the honeysuckle's hedge
>   Pipes the green linnet."

True Nature lover !—to feel the impulse of the great
mother's heart beat thus !

To that sublime and richly-endowed but early-fated
poet, Shelley, the phosphorescence of the glow-worm
was no more unfamiliar than the rich flood of melody
that bursts from the skylark, or he'd ne'er have written—

> " Like a glow-worm golden,
>   In a dell of dew
>   Scattering unbeholden
>   Its aerial hue
> Among the flowers and grass which screen it from the view."
> —*Ode to a Skylark.*

But it was long before these noted songsters spoke in "rounded numbers smooth" that the mark of a scientific imagination enriched the pages of poetry; for that master of English verse and criticism, John Dryden (who established the Alexandrine metre), evinced a scientific training. Here was a man to whom science or any other faculty was unknown; he simply held the mirror up to nature, and his verses therein reflected the images opposed to it. His works abound in knowledge and sparkle with illustration. Yes, it was Dryden who built up English song, refined its language, and corrected its sentiments. No source of information was foreign to him, for he consulted both the living and the dead. We need only look to "Palamon and Arcite" to trace the author's knowledge of embryology, to give him credit for knowing the early stages of man's development in portraying the unit of society :—

> " So man, at first a drop, dilates with heat,
> Then, formed, his little heart begins to beat;
> Secret he feeds, unknowing, in the cell ;
> At length, for hatching ripe, he breaks the shell,
> And struggles into breath, and cries for aid,
> Then, helpless, in his mother's lap is laid."
>
> —Book iii., line 1066.

Dryden clearly hints that the human ovum—a mysterious speck of protoplasm—is endowed with a faculty of segmentation and differentiation ere it is evolved into man's complex organism.

But there was another poet who bandied epigram with Byron, was a friend of Southey, a contemporary of Wordsworth, Coleridge, and Scott, in the fulness of

whose genius the swift and shining transits of Shelley
and Keats shone out like shooting-stars—I mean Walter
Savage Landor : he surveyed the realm of nature from
a scientific standpoint ; trees, flowers, man, beast, and
every creeping thing were sacred to him, and full of
happy life, for it was his wont—

> " To let all flowers live freely and all die,
>   Whene'er their genius bids their souls depart,
>   Among their kindred ;
>   I never pluck the rose, the violet's head
>   Hath shaken with my breath upon its bank,
>   And not reproached me ; the ever sacred cups
>   Of the pure lily have between my hands
>   Felt safe, unsoiled, nor lost one grain of gold."

But to pass by this brilliant but caustic writer ! However bitter and long-sustained the conflict between faith
and science, however numerous the traditions that must
yield to the advances of knowledge, there is no anta-
gonism between science and poetry ; the champion of
the latter then may take courage in Poe's words and
march under the banner of a new crusade, albeit science
has "dragged Diana from her car," "driven the Hama-
dryad from the wood," although she has torn "the Naiad
from the flood," and the "elfin from the green grass."
But although poetry has been robbed of all these myths,
she can now avail herself of the more resplendent beauty
of discovered truth, she can now light the flames of her
fancy at the torch which science carries aloft. It was
Landor, of whom I have just spoken, who said that
"much of what we call sublime is only the residue of
infancy," and there is no doubt that so far from being

unfriendly, science will breathe into poetry a fresher life. Men may talk of the "celestial flowers that strew heaven's path," but we know this to be but metaphor—a childish idle password. We know that all that glorious iridescence about the sun to be but refraction of white light in its passage through space: we thus understand Landor's statement!

Though art and fashion may change again and again, the pure office of poetry is to idealise and prophesy of the great unknown, to shadow forth, in glimpses though it be, hints of the soul of nature; and in spite of much of the tinsel being removed from the ancient idol, there is no reason to believe that the poet's office is to suffer, but that the rather it will become enriched as time rolls on, and for this reason, that man's nature and his needs have not changed. It is certain that science can, and largely does, kindle the imagination into new creations, and hereby proves itself the muse's ally; it is equally certain that the poet often anticipates the discoveries of the *savants* concerning the laws of mind and being. Before the nature of light and the correlation of forces were discovered, we find Goethe avow that—

> " Light, however it weaves,
>   Still, fettered, unto bodies cleaves;
>   It flows from bodies, bodies beautifies;
>   By bodies is its course impeded."

That unequal yet strayed minstrel of the early Victorian era, Beddoes, when he wrote "Death's Jest Book," fore-shadowed a truth that was to occupy later on the mind of the apostle of organic evolution, when he said—

" I have a bit of *Fiat* in my soul,
And can myself create my little world ;
Had I been born a four-legged thing, methinks
I might have formed the steps from dog to man,
And crept into his nature."

This writer clearly hints at progressive development—
mind springing from inert matter, through the crystal,
through the plant, through all life, up to man, the paragon
of animals ; in other words, evolution guides his thoughts
as the method of the world's sustentation.   And if this was
written in the thirties, what must be the feeling of men
in the nineties ? Must they not feel dazed by the posses-
sion of a new sense, or what is the use of the novel and
sublime objects revealed by the lens, the laboratory, and
the other instruments of science ? Surely they have cause
to rejoice in a new life, for our latter-day knowledge must
be taken into account : it is idle to think that poets will
rest content with ignoring or lightly passing over what
has become everyday matter of fact. As Stedman says :
" The spiritual domain is still the poet's own ; but let his
interpretations be derived from living truths, rather than
from the worn and ancient fables of a pastoral age."   Of
all knowledge, then, poetry is the first and last ; it is first,
in that imagination always carves the way to the discovery of truth—that theories forestall facts ; it is last, in
that it enshrines the beauty of truth in the language of
the soul. Whatever revolution men of science may bring
about, the disciples of verse will incorporate it into their
system of imagery ; ancient interpretations of the muse
may have to assume new drapery, but the proportions of
the fair goddess will have to be respected in a new year

of grace. So the poet of the future must neither slumber nor sleep, but, like a true lover of his art, he must follow the steps of his learned brother—never content till he shall have hallowed with the magic of his art the new sources of inspiration at his command; for what was said so felicitously by Wordsworth in this connection still holds good: "If the time should ever come when science shall be ready to put on a new form of flesh and blood, the poet will lend his divine spirit to aid the transfiguration."

Without that special gift, the imagination, which is the life and the light of the cultured man, there would be no common ground on which to dispute the claims of science or poetry; but it is this power that enables a child to understand an axiom in Euclid, as much as it is the power that leads the investigator from one step to another; and so, in a way, the minds of a Milton and a Huxley are akin—enjoy a common bond of sympathy.

The facts that I have attempted to embody under "Stellar Songs" may by some be accounted wanting in imagery, but I must plead that had I paid more attention to ornament, the structure and the matter would have suffered in truth. I have deemed it essential to preserve in so abstruse a subject the narrative form, and be true to fact rather than to fancy. In unfolding the physical laws of the universe, the salient features must appeal to the mind rather than to the imagination, which is its playground. It must be granted, then, that it is better to utter a truth in plain language than to indulge in a poetical rhapsody! The reader must pass on for themes rich in the labour of polish, and touched with

the finish of passion. It is impossible to be always equal
and invariably adequate in writing, so should the matter
be deemed faulty, I would adjure the reader to pass
quickly on—as over thin ice.

Equally I may be deemed guilty of a sustained classical
and metrical oration, in spite of which, or attempting
which, I would remind my accuser of the great truths
and transcendent interest underlying my theme. We
cannot unfold that which is dark to ordinary vision
without something suffering, unless we are befriended
by a perfect language, a most orderly government, and
an unmolested environment. If we discuss the laws that
regulate our being, we should do so from the point of
reason, blending as much imagery as the situation will
permit, not, contrariwise, give an imaginary rendering of
things, heedless of cause or relation. I have endeavoured,
then, to interpret some of the great truths embodied in
the writings of various astronomers, from an outer as
well as from an inner aspect: the immensity of the task
has grown with its progress, and the deficiencies have
become still more apparent as fuller light and inquiry
have enriched the subject. The march past—the reading
of such an array of facts as I have adduced, would be
intolerable at a sitting, in prose; it is for this reason, and
to stimulate a love for astronomy, that I have adopted
the didactic form of poetry in a six-lined hexameter—the
interrupted measure followed by the complete couplet.

From what has gone before, from the copious illustra-
tions I have given of the relations between science and
poetry, from the fact that a training in the natural
sciences, and long continued habits of life in company

with men of research, have not tended to efface the expressions of a poetical temperament, it will be conceded that both subjects may be congenial and common to the same mind.

A knowledge of science and its pursuits, if not too exclusive, instead of blighting, tends to foster and enlarge the range of a poet's sympathy. I say this, because it is often maintained that fact-grinding destroys the poetical sentiments. Whoever has read that sparkling American's writings, the prose and poetical works of O. W. Holmes, will see an instance of the zest and relish with which professional men from time to time betake themselves to the pen rather than to the scalpel. Steeped in the lore of a hard and dry calling, and teaching the very secrets of man's frame in the charnel-house of science, he can afford to write as daintily as he does tersely, dilate on the virtues of a deceased sire as on the "Stability of Science." What could be more pathetic than—

> " The mossy markles rest
> On the lips that he has prest
> In their bloom,
> And the names he loved to hear
> Have been carved for many a year
> On the tomb.
> My grandmamma has said—
> Poor old lady, she is dead
> Long ago—
> That he had a Roman nose,
> And his cheek was like the rose
> In the snow."—*The Last Leaf.*

Speaking of science, what could be more terse and classical than—

" The Greek, the Roman, reared its ancient walls
  In that fair niche, by countless billows laved,
  Trace the deep lines that Sydenham engraved ;
  On yon broad front that breasts the changing swell,
  Mark where the ponderous sledge of Hunter fell ! "
  —*The Stability of Science.*

Nor does poetry suffer in such men's hands ! Because
a man knows such a science as medicine, is he dis-
qualified for taking up the poet's pen ? Absurd ! Or
take another case. Because one knows the physics of
the sun, does it diminish by one iota my feeling of joy
on witnessing the orb of day rise from the Khin-gan
Mountains ? Did it diminish the above author's regard
for science when he wrote—

" Go to yon tower, where busy science plies
  Her vast antennæ, feeling through the skies ;
  That little vernier, on whose slender lines
  The midnight taper trembles as it shines,
  A silent index tracks the planets' march
  In all their wanderings through the ethereal arch,
  Tells through the mist where dazzled Mercury burns,
  And marks the spot where Uranus returns."
  —*Urania.* Delivered at Boston, 1846.

Yet there are men who say such training as Holmes's
stifles poetical feelings and expressions ! We loiter
down the lane and gaze on nature's carpet of green, but
because we know the form and structure of the daisy, is
our love for the little composite flower diminished ?

So with the perfume and colour of other flowers ; because we have Henslow and Lubbock at our fingers'
ends, and are acquainted with flower-fertilisation, is it
a reason why our love of the beautiful should suffer ?

Equally with our knowledge of physiography, of dew;
can the freshness of the mind as of the morning air be
lost, or its sweetness abate, through the light inquiry
has given us respecting those "infant diamonds that
bespangle the blades of grass"? Is not rather their
charm increased by such knowledge? As Wilson says:
"The hues of the shell tost up at our feet enchant us
through the colour-sense, and beauty of form and shape
appeal eloquently to us as parts of the poetry of nature!"
And all this in spite of our knowledge of the principles of
light and the laws of morphology, the poetry investing
the once sailing little craft still lives on! And so with
flowers; our acquaintance with their natural order, genus,
and habitat diminishes not the pride we take in our
gardens. Because the structure and function of such an
organ as the larynx is as familiar to us as is our alphabet,
we no less enjoy the notes of a Norma or the glorious
song that echoes through the cathedral transept; our
souls are equally aroused heavenwards, and our hearts
keep pace to the same chords of sympathy that are
awakened in the religious. One might as well assert
that our sense of the lovely in music is chilled by a
knowledge of musical laws, or say that because we
are versed in the philosophy of secretions, we are
indifferent to a beautiful woman's tears, or fail to be
touched by them! And many other instances arise,
such as our acquaintance with Bell "On the Hand,"
for here we do not lose sense of the poetry investing
that eloquent member; nor did Browning lose his
regard for scientific precision—on the contrary, with the
anatomist—

" To him the bones their inmost secret yield,　　　. . .
　Each notch and nodule signify their use ;
　On him the muscles turn in triple tier,
　And pleasantly inspire the entrusted man."

So that we may say with confidence that science does
not destroy the sense of beauty, or blight the function of
poetry; for, as we have seen with our modern poets,
their very art is strengthened with a fuller wisdom; and
though the grave of many a myth and superstition is
brought about, we are but entering the land of a better
birth. All this, it may be said, is very optimistic, and
truly so, but then poetry is the art of arts, and sustains
our highest and best faculties.

The tendency of a too exclusive attention to science
has always been to blight and stunt the instinct for the
muse, but this is because the handmaid (poetry) has not
waited faithfully, in the intervals of human enterprise, on
the proud master—Reason! Too great a devotion to
science, as Miss F. Power Cobbe has well said, tends
to wither our higher faculties of mind, for " Reverence,
sympathy, and modesty dwindle in its shadow, art and
poetry shrink at its touch, morality is undermined by it,
and religion perishes at its approach." All this means
that man, being a many-sided creature, must not exercise
one faculty at the expense of another, for disuse means
decay! Turning from Miss Cobbe—who is always on
the war-path against science, as the champion of religion
and morality—let us hear what that hopeful and deeply-
read student and master of English literature, Mr. J. A.
Symonds, says: " In our days science is more vitally
poetical than art, for it opens wider horizons than verse.

. . . Yet there are not wanting signs which justify a
sober critic in predicting that our enthusiasm for nature
is but the prelude to a more majestic poetry, combining
truth with faith, and fact with fiction."

The intuition that characterises the normal being is
adverse to any association between the two realms; it
teaches—"I must see science unbefriended by sentiment; I must have poetry unchilled by the cold precision of science!" The larger reflective faculty, however,
holds forth, and will continue to proclaim, that poetry
shorn of truth, and notably that outlined by reason, is
not a representative poetry. Of course the singer may
equally abound in lofty strains and as full a measure of
song, but the music will not arouse the enthusiasm of
the cultured listener, or be as calculated to stay with the
reader of it. The exact mode of viewing nature does
not destroy or annul the sense whereby we detect its
external beauty; no! or that wondrous and subtle
rhythm—spirit, if you will—that pervades the universe
at large.

So long as literature lasts, and in spite of modern
advances in human enterprise generally, it is my pleasure
to predict that poetry will continue to vibrate through
man's better nature—although a great living statesman
says, No! as the expression of his deepest emotion, as
the reflex of his inmost mind. Should it ever fall into
decay, the spirit of literature will be dead, and man's
soul despoiled of one of its richest treasures; for without its hallowing influences the ring of rapture and the
tremulo of delight that fill the finely-strung bosom will
have no expression, and the "dress of thought" which

the cultured man assumes be deprived of beauty: the song of triumph, the pæan of joy, "the voice that breathed o'er Eden," the lament for the dead—"He giveth His beloved sleep!"—in the absence of poetry would inadequately burst forth, and a world of charm and interest exist without an interpreter! Under its genial influence man is led to a fairer vision of things, his beauty-sense is kept in tune, and the "thousand strings of life" acquire a meaning. Poetry is the fairy that beguiles him in life "whenever its way seems long," that bids him take courage "when his heart begins to fail!" The cry of its utility has gone forth, and if its cause is invertebrate from an intellectual point of view, none can gainsay its power as a mighty lever to develop, buoy up, and sustain the moral side of man's nature. What would the literature of the world be without the writings of Homer, Æschylus, Milton, and Goethe?— yea, of Isaiah, Thomas à Kempis, Herbert, and even Shakespeare, with a host of others? The lofty imagery in mind and morals, and the sublime language that appeals to both mind and heart that such men have made immortal, tell their own tale, and show that poetry as the expression of the deepest thoughts and emotions of man can never fade! for in her mighty scroll are enshrined the ethics of the bygone ages, and the noblest sentiments that humanity can express. It is the office of poetry to pourtray whatever is true and whatever is beautiful, and to make the true and the beautiful subserve each other. Fashions may change, faiths grow apace, and finally wane because unfitted to depict the truer aspects of life, and the thoughts of God which

c

the progress of time unfolds; but poetry, so long as it blends truth and beauty together, will never die.   As Keats says—

> " Beauty is truth, truth beauty ! that is all
>   We know on earth, and all we need to know ! "
> > —*Ode to a Grecian Urn.*

When religion and science shall have kissed each other, when science and poetry shall have embarked as boon companions in the same craft on the great ocean of Truth—then, and not till then, shall we have reason to expect glimpses of that long spoken of but distant millennium in civilisation; then, alone, can we hope to see realised the poet's glorious prophecy, when he said—

> " Then shall the reign of Mind commence on earth,
>   And, starting fresh as from some second birth,
>   Man, in the sunshine of the world's new spring,
>   Shall walk, transparent like some holy thing !
>   Then, too, your Prophet from his angel brow
>   Shall cast the veil that hides its splendours now,
>   And gladdened earth shall through her wide expanse
>   Bask in the glories of this countenance."
> > —*Lalla Rookh.*

PART I.

Stellar Songs.

(AN ASTRONOMICAL STUDY.)

PROEM.

'TWAS in October, when with rustling fall
   The sere and yellow leaves hied to the lawn,
When the effulgent sun began to pall
   That glads the heart of man from early dawn,
That I essayed the lofty task with glee
Of this romance of " how things came to be ! "

No mind that's fettered must dare pierce this veil
   Of mystery, no prejudice man's soul
Must fondle ; childhood's simple fairy tale
   Must slumber as unfolds my mystic scroll ;
Then come with me, and Truth shall be our guide,
And proud Minerva ever by our side !

We will invoke the muse on the sublime
   And glorious story of the heavens, the play—
The rhythmic flight of worlds, pourtray how Time
   And Mass the Cosmos framed, the Milky Way,
The reign of law in Meteors we will trace,
And illustrate the realms they help to grace !

CHAPTER I.

I.

THE last beams of the setting sun had tinged
    The horizon's western vault—the moon had risen
In crescent form, its earthly face being fringed
    With borrowed rays alone; abaft the mizen,
While pacing lordly deck, I saw afar,
Course the ethereal planes, a shooting star !

II.

Whence didst thou come, gay flashing meteor?
    What force propelled thee through the sea of space?
Didst thou collide with fellow-mate there, or
    Were thy bright sparks created by thy pace?
Was it a might—repulsive from the sun,
That lit thy fused spray as thy body spun?

III.

Thy lustre, track electric, cometh nigh
    To brilliancy of comet; in thy flight
Eccentric, in thy awful plunge, the eye
    Of telescope can't follow thee at night;
Like some bark shipwrecked in tempestuous plane,
With tail afire, thou seem'st, then lost again.

IV.

What power thy mighty swoop once lent
  Volcanic monarch of abyss, or star
Worn out by age, disintegrated, rent
  Into the vapoury void, is more by far
Than pen can tell! Thy parabolic course
Makes thee a tourist of all realms perforce!

V.

What is thy composition? Hast thou weight,
  Extension like this little world of ours?
Or dost thou float like cork, or is thy state
  One like to lava molten? Of the flowers
Spangling the heavens, fancy assumes thy light,
Thy tail's of phosphorus ablaze at night!

VI.

While thy bright nucleus is formed we know
  Of elements akin to those on earth
—Welded and petrified, and free from glow—
  All this we gather from thy death, not birth;
And so thou weight possessest we can say,
Though doubt hangs o'er the nature of thy spray!

VII.

Thou art a waif, then, of some distant star,
  The shipwrecked scion of some giant orb,
Hurled to vast depths, to elements afar,
  Till gravitation, heat, thy powers absorb!
Part gaseous is thy nature—through thy speed,
Part solid—facts which " he who runs may read "!

VIII.

Thy composition then's no secret found ;
　But what about thy flight, thy headlong fate,
Afar from the earth's atmosphere?　No sound
　Follows thy swoop, to gauge thy speed at all,
Save when thou till'st the earth, when Etna's blast
Eruptive 's child's-play to thy havoc vast !

IX.

Restless activity is thine, transcendent speed,
　Engine of travel or of arms can't touch !
Thy streak of splendour can alone proceed
　From course arrested ; transformation such
As man sees in thy vaporous display
Can only be produced in such a way !

X.

Unless thy force centripetal thee led
　So near the sun, that melted thou became
A molten ball of fire with granules shed
　As thy tail's retinue, a train of flame—
Figures all fail, man can't thy speed compare,
Except to lightning flashing through the air !

XI.

But for thy tour, in part illumined thus
　Through speed, collision, journey near the sun,
Thy course had never been revealed to us,
　Thy flight had ne'er our admiration won !
Changed though thy form, thy energy's the same,
Nothing is lost—either by fire or flame !

XII.

The laws of conservation tolerate,
   Nothing created suddenly or lost!
The elements alone but shift their state;
   The flow of power is constant, though oft tost
Like ocean surf about; the waves may change
To ripples, these to angry waves may range.

XIII.

The sun, for instance, may dry up in space
   A planet full of life, and turn to moon
The energy it had—to form new race;
   Or cast it forth as comet—late at noon
Afire near earth! The fund of cosmic power
Is constant in the sunshine, in the shower!

XIV.

The stately pageantry of mighty globes,
   The galaxy of glory in the lights
Of queenly stars, Aurora's glorious robes,
   The shower of meteors on November nights,
Luna's fresh phase, the eccentric comet's course,
Are modulations of the same fixed force!

XV.

Such is the principle that governs space—
   Planets roll on, wielding their precious freight
Phœbus around! 'Tis only when the face—
   The veil of earth—is struck through force and weight
Of falling stars, thought dwells on nature's laws,
And man affects to seek the salvo's cause!

XVI.

The roar of cannon and the lightning's flash
  Pall on the mind before the sound and light
Of transformation scene of meteors' crash,
  Which oft drench cities with their hail at night
And flood of glitter !   Thunderstorm is dumb
Beside the fire-ball striking earth's air plumb !

XVII.

Seek out a plateau on a winter's night,
  Or mountain vantage-ground, anticipate
A coming meteor's fall, and such a sight
  (November showers are always true to date)
As glow effulgent of electric lamp
Can't equal, will attend you at your camp.

XVIII.

Or, come another night, be raging fall of snow
  And darkness dense, above, around, the scene
A transformation soon will undergo,
  (While meteors swiftly wing the sky, I mean,)
A track of fusing fire will flood the land,
And strike you as a panorama grand !

XIX.

In its career—so mad, so terrible—
  The falling star is pulverised, dissolved
To dust, to lambent sparks—made visible
  As pencil through its speed ; the tail's resolved
Into a fiery spray, so poised in air
As to give brilliant flash, if night be fair !

XX.

And though the meteors shiver in their pace
   Through planes of empyrean, that the eye
Is dazzled, trick'd, as many seem to chase
   Each other in fresh orbit through the sky,
The echo of their thunder's only heard
When the ball strikes our atmosphere is inferred !

XXI.

No matter what its source, its energy
   Continues till its motion is destroyed ;
Like modern engine, the machinery
   Giving it passage, but propels in void
With constant impetus the mass ; its flight
Holds on till governor is wrecked outright !

XXII.

Disintegration—falling of the star
   The earth against, equilibration lends
The meteor's fate !   All things are on a par :
   Youth totters into age ; the flower that sends
The sweetest fragrance out, withers and dies ;
Vast empires fall !   Such are the destinies !

XXIII.

'Tis on the western continent the stream
   Of lurid brilliants such dire havoc plays ;
Here all their throes of dissolution seem
   The meteors to expend in mighty blaze,
As though the death of flying matter here
Is calculated to inspire less fear !

XXIV.

Dazzling, perplexing is the spectacle
 That meets the eye ; gay troops of brilliants march
Across the heavens, as though no obstacle
 The balls of fire while spangling heaven's arch
Could meet, when, detonation dire ! a blast
Like unto dynamite afire comes fast !

XXV.

For, be the meteor but in weight a pound,
 It travels five-and-twenty miles—while one's
Being counted—rate for which no round
 Or charge can be expressed, except in tons.
No gun is found the meteoric speed
To millimetre meet when charge is freed !

XXVI.

Such of a single ball, but clusters oft
 Of beautiful design evolve from mass,
When fell explosion shivers them aloft.
 Such was the case with meteors at Kansas,
When rent asunder Mississippi near,
After a thousand miles of mad career.

XXVII.

In eighteen seventy-six Niagara's Falls
 Were silenced by the explosion, by the noise
Of pent up energy of scattered balls
 Set free so suddenly ; the equipoise
Of static force evoked so dire a shock,
That people thought it was an earthquake's rock !

XXVIII.

The heavens shone like day, Luna's pale lamp
   Well-nigh went out in Indiana State,
Such was the glow at night ! " men left their camp
   And sojourned home—trains ran at usual rate."
The world jogged on in peace, when through the air
A blast terrific sounded everywhere !

XXIX.

" 'Twas the pace that killed ! "—Titanic power
   Once lent the meteor bolt—majestic throe
In finding dissolution ! 'Twas the shower
   Of mass against a rival force aglow !
The missile shed its glory in its course,
Through the surrender of a mighty force !

XXX.

But more about the meteoric cloud !
   Whence comes the pearl-white luminosity ?
The light of falling stars is not endowed
   With power to pierce dense air's humidity.
Then why is track aglow at dead of night,
If brilliancy is not reflected light ?

XXXI.

'Tis that the meteor, pensioned by the sun
   With ghostlike property in times gone by,
Has been ignited as the body spun,
   And shone apace through clouds though overcast !
Some phosphorescent atoms have been stored
In brilliants' mass, then back to space restored !

XXXII.

The sun's resources—what a splendid theme !—
 Illimitable are : planets and space,
Mapped out by Copernic upon his stream,
 His flood of light depend ! the human race,
On Sol's beneficence solely subsists,
Tempered through vapour to *its* interests !

CHAPTER II.

XXXIII.

Author of Time, creator of the tides !
    Imperial lord of space—of every plane
Known unto men ! of planets grand besides,
    The fire-crowned monarch with his flaming train
Dispenses night and day, sets forth the noon,
And rules the seasons as he doth each moon !

XXXIV.

Meridians, too vast to comprehend,
    Drink in his beams of radiance, tiny motes
Wandering in space, as well as orbs that wend
    Their stately course !   To each plane Sol devotes
A meed of glory ; building up a globe,
Or life there limning, in some glorious robe.

XXXV.

But vast as is the heat, each moment spent—
    A store that equal is to boiling down
Twelve thousand million miles of ice, that lent
    Unto the orb of Life's too weak to own
Beside the mass—a millimetre clear,
Won't tell the share poor Tellus gets a year !

XXXVI.

The life-inspiring heat yet shed below
    Through veil eternal, rules both wind and wave,
Climates and seasons; races on its glow
    Depend!—all life on to the grave!
The icy sleep of death that knows no morn
Comes from our breath of solar beams being shorn!

XXXVII.

The clouds of vapour that ascend at dawn
    Obey the magnet of the solar rays
Ere they're condensed, to fall upon the lawn
    As drops of rain, or frozen snow, or haze.
Thus glaciers on the Alps mount to the sky,
Till melted seawards, seeking gravity.

XXXVIII.

Sol thus absorbs, gives back an equal wealth
    Of life-promoting dew, rich with his dower—
The germs of growth!   He rivers lifts by stealth,
    And streamlets to the ocean by his power!
Thus by the sun's Atlantean, Titan pull
Are shallows emptied, oceans too made full!

XXXIX.

The subtle act whereby the young plant grows,
    Appropriates its food, comes from the play
Of solar beams; it chooses atoms, throws
    Those foreign to it to the winds away!
So twigs assume their robes in floral realm,
Cells multiply by carbon—towers the elm!

D

XL.

Tint-loving cells are nourished then, and breathes
   Freely the blade, digesting all it can
Of oxygen, till ripened are the sheaves
   At harvest-tide, till fruits are rich in tan !
So stored-up sunbeams represent the good
Of solar influence—we've daily food !

XLI.

The varying climes, the currents of the sea,
   Cyclones and calms together, find their cause
In sunny light and heat ;—man's energy
   And that of all life emanates from laws
Adaptively decreed and meted out
By the Fire-King the universe throughout !

XLII.

All vital force is thus traced back to rays
   Once pent up in the sun ; man's genius
From muscle of the kine's built up, and cattle graze
   Upon the verdant blades made vigorous
By solar bounty,—beams dispensed to soil
Make seedlings fructify through summer toil !

XLIII.

Realms in the womb of space—no eye can see,
   No lens can reach—banquet from day to day
Upon Sol's beams ! life, in immensity
   Yet nobler, feeds upon his torch, I say !
He worlds unknown sustains from age to age,
Thunder and lightning are his equipage !

XLIV.

The Queen of Night from first to fullest phase
   Owes all her lustrous glory to the light—
Lent by Apollo's lamp—to deck her face ;
   And so with planets 'tis, that shine at night,
Yet twinkle not !—their splendour, every one,
Comes from the effulgence of the regal sun !

XLV.

The broad thick-studded road that shines with gold,
   Whose pavements jewelled with starlets rich in light,
May myriad forms of life with beauty mould
   Beyond the milky constellation bright ;
But no force rules a retinue of worlds
Like unto that of Sol, such wealth unfurls !

XLVI.

The warmth imparted by the flickering fire
   That lights the palace, glads the peasant's soul
On long, cold, cheerless nights of winter dire,
   Comes from beam-laden forests turned to coal
In æons gone !—from fossilised remains
Of woods, luxuriant in primeval plains !

XLVII.

Gigantic ferns and forests that have drunk
   In carbon from Sol's radiance, till a store
Of rays has fully clothed them, which have sunk
   Into the vasty deep for man t' explore
In future age. Yes ! treasures rich in beams
For ages hidden, till restored from seams !

XLVIII.

So with the light, the artificial glow—
   Gaseous, electric, this is but a source
Of solar energy, long hid below
   In miles of coal dissolved—an ebon force ;
A store of bounty, treasured till to-day,
Hungry for oxygen to burn away !

XLIX.

The fleecy clouds ere they're surcharged with rain,
   And fall by gravitation to the earth,
Owe all their beauty to th' beams they obtain
   From heaven's lamp ; for cumuli gain birth
From vaporous oceans, swelling as they rise,
And being festooned with glory in the skies !

L.

The fuel that feeds the forge, the beacon's glow,
   The wind-tost light that glads the adventurer's camp,
Is but a bounteous force long lent below,—
   One day to be repaid—by the great lamp,
The light of day, whose beams alone complete
The varied forms of life through solar heat.

LI.

The same power lifts evaporation's spray,
   And heavenward tends the " water dust " to draw
Ere the next force—cohesion—'gins to play
   Upon the risen vapour, when the law
Of gravitation hurries to the plain
Below the vapour—in the form of rain.

LII.

Behold Sol's spectrum in the coloured bow
　That decks the heavens in an arch of tint—
A ring of promise—till the colours glow
　In radiant bands of beauty without stint !
The fertile rain—the angel of the sea,
Reflects its sevenfold luminosity !

LIII.

The force that nurtures e'en the growing chick,
　That paints the gaudy peacock in its grace,
That prompts the restless steed to plunge and kick
　Ere the lithe sportman's mounted for the race,
Alike proceed from elements of food
By sunbeams built up for the common good !

LIV.

The berry perfected in Mocha's soil,
　Whose tonic essence elevates the frame
When drawn without by water " on the boil ; "
　The nectar—tea—that cheers both maid and dame,
But ne'er inebriates, like to water's due
To Sol's beneficence, resources too !

LV.

The seasons, meted to man's wants, next prove
　His bounteous dispensation throughout space,
Whether the orb be tilted—poised to move
　In axis to or from his glowing face ;
Winter and summer typify his ray,
Setting or rising marks his night or day !

LVI.

Realms unexplorèd, races too unknown,
   Planes of eternal day, and voids profound
Drink in his beams while basking 'neath his throne,
   And every planet in its merry round
Luxuriates in its course—each living soul
Feeds on his garnered fruits from pole to pole.

CHAPTER III.

LVII.

Who'd grasp the stately laws adjusting worlds
    Mighty in magnitude, must learn the play
Of atoms cast adrift—the meteor 'tis unfurls
    The secrets of the cosmos, leads the way
To the mind's grip of planets small and grand :
He stellar problems, then, can understand.

LVIII.

Now heaven's vault, abundance of small stars
    Scattered at random from some crater's brim,
Eccentric course to steer, the gates unbars
    Of chance ;—'tis from examples small men limn
The drama of spectacular events,
Transits of Venus—Sol's magnificence !

LIX.

Like to the wand of harlequin, the streak
    Crescentic of the meteor appears
At times aglow, a state we'll try to seek
    A reason ; now the lava as it nears
The lofty heights of atmosphere is bent
By virtue of the vapour it has rent.

55

LX.

Pelted on all sides by these lively hosts,
  The world has still jogged on with here a wreck
And there a shock—the universal coasts
  Have been bestrewn with ashes, but no check
Has that proud pilot suffered on his way,
The helmsman, Gravitation, to this day!

LXI.

Varieties of meteors are found,
  That we must now endeavour to discuss;
Legions, the size of grains of sand, abound,
  A few descend as bright as Sirius;
Battalions of fourth magnitude outright
Exceed the first, bright as the star of night.

LXII.

Comparisons of splendour, understand,
  Are directed to the nucleus aglow;
The scale of size, proximity to land
  We dwell on, is relation we should know:
Men on stars of Luna's lustre have oft gazed,
And falling lights as bright as Jove have blazed!

LXIII.

Thus though meteors diverse preponderate
  At a given tour of planet's round, those seen
Are but a fraction of the army great,
  Sweeping their courses in the planes serene.
Unplumbed profounds of space receive the glow
Of countless millions as they, wandering, go.

LXIV.

In the silence of the night the study lends
   The glories of the heavens a fitness wise ;
'Tis only when the falling meteor rends
   The atmosphere that murmur doth arise ;
Call of owl and water-hen may sometimes break
The calm, or heron's note from tranquil lake.

LXV.

The meteor, like the lover lorn, astray,
   With its favour to eclipse the stars of night,
For triumph rests upon unfettered way,
   Clear ocean, calm, and freedom in its flight :
'Tis the rivalry, the struggle in the skies,
That wrecks the calm, the beauty of its eyes.

LXVI.

For given states oft hinder the displays
   Of gay and flashing meteors' candent beams ;
Diana, Queen of Night, in her late phase
   Their glory may impair.   The shooting stars
May too by floating clouds be neutralised—
The veil whereby Sol's face is oft disguised.

LXVII.

There was a time when human destinies
   Were ruled by the caprices of the stars,
When fates were told through Luna's kind decree,
   And victory followed the consent of Mars :
Men staggered at events, but sought no cause ;
Now everything depends on Natural Laws !

LXVIII.

And so it comes about this planet swings
   At stated periods—as long ago—
Into the shoal of hurtling stars, and flings
   Each off, as through the Archipelago
Called "Leonids" it steers—the great shower's pelt
Is once alone in thirty-three years felt !

LXIX.

Leo, "the Lion," constellation bold !
   Marks out the spot, though far behind the site
Of " Leonids "—as through the heavens, we're told,
   The universe of wealth shoots out its light—
The mighty column on the fourteenth day
Of month the last but one makes its display.

LXX.

Shaped like a continent of slender girth,
   The gay parade of glowing hosts flies past
The shadowed sun-forsaken coasts of earth
   To greet the face of man ; the length's too vast
To set to verse's measure—though the shower
Travels at ninety thousand miles an hour.

LXXI.

The width—the curious may ask—of shoal
   'S one hundred thousand miles from either side,
Or that of earth's span quadrupled from pole
   To pole ; the awful length's then multiplied
By fifteen thousand—computations, such,
As simple mortals must bewilder much.

LXXII.

Like an imperial racecourse, rich in steeds,
  The mighty continent of meteors steers
Through th' empyrean in fell swoop, that needs
  Must intersect some orb's course, as it nears
The humbler revolution.   Hence the plane
Of this Earth's cut through in the shower's campaign !

LXXIII.

But all the cannonading in the event
  Of this collision by the mighty shoal,
Tilting the face of Earth, 's incompetent
  To sway the stately planet in its roll !
Like a top spinning on a sharp incline,
The shower its orbit cannot undermine.

LXXIV.

Brushed on all sides by meteors in their flight
  Across its path, the air-clad globe hies on,
Wrecking the glowing units that alight
  With swiftness its dense atmosphere upon :
Destruction dire and sudden is the doom
Of brilliant missiles as they downwards loom !

LXXV.

The years roll on, the ranks in bright array
  March past, discomfited through sea of space,
Till globe of life's completely cut its way,
  And from the troop celestial turned its face :
Another revolution nearly rids
This world of dazzle of the " Leonids."

LXXVI.

For sixteen years the " Leonids " now scour
 The depths of space in parabolic curve,
Orbs' planes bisecting; stellar worlds their shower
 Of glory shedding o'er till time to swerve
Back to the coasts of earth and solar source :
Half of their journey's now attained perforce !

LXXVII.

The straggling tail, after the second year,
 Has vanished, flashed, the mighty guard's advanced,—
Proceeded on its tour—in spite of rear
 Contingents faltering, it may be, entranced
A nobler race of men on nobler sphere,
Maybe played havoc with its atmosphere !

LXXVIII.

On to the number of a hundred whirl
 Systems of meteors our Earth around,
Of which the brilliant Pleiades unfurl
 The next approaching glory in their round
Of wild ellipse—Andromedes, a shoal
Of fainter splendour, follows in the roll !

LXXIX.

But great as is the meteors' storm, man's life
 Is seldom sacrificed, though authors say
Four hundred millions fall with havoc rife
 Per hour on earth, at rate no musketry
Can imitate in speed—protection rests
Upon the atmosphere the globe invests !

LXXX.

What untold meteoric wealth must deck
   Infinity of space, if thus, throughout,
With fleeting lights as numerous as that speck—
   That microcosm—Earth, 'tis decked about !
Yet gravitation guides each diverse group ;
Both void and matter to its laws must stoop !

LXXXI.

The smallest speck that in a sunbeam floats
   Obeys the same law as the falling star ;
The motion-wielding Luna, like the motes,
   Is just the same as planets that afar
In mighty orbits' whirl are governed by :
'Tis gravitation's sole supremacy !

LXXXII.

There was a time when Earth the centre was
   Of planetary motion, was the orb
Of central power, when the laborious
   Data of Kepler men's minds came to absorb,
Which showed that planets in ellipses roll
Around the sun—all flattened at the pole !

LXXXIII.

The shape oblate arose when swing began
   Of orb, when semi-solid—therefore prone
Beneath the force centripetal of sun
   To swell out at circumference alone ;
'Tis through its axis that the sun, its might
Meted through poles, the orb directs in flight !

LXXXIV.

To be attracted by a larger mass
   Is units' tendency—hence planets have
Magnetic force, which tempts them all to pass
   Into their source.   'Tis the repulsive wave,
Exerted by the sun that keeps in place
Each finished planet, as it rolls in space !

LXXXV.

From his rich casket the next gem of thought
   That Kepler's ingenuity rolled out
Was, that the chain 'tween sun and planet ought
   To swing like pendulum in space about—
Passing as in a wheel o'er given spokes
In equal time, in never-varying strokes !

LXXXVI.

Then came the law linking the planets all
   Into one giant chain by bonds, as wise
As simple, which sets forth the numeral
   Telling the planet's orbit in the skies
To multiplied by self be ; when the whole
Will bear proportion to the planet's roll !

LXXXVII.

But what about the roll?   Well, this
   Must twice be multiplied ere figures show
Its rate to distance—such discoveries
   As clearly tell us how the planets go ;
With distance their attraction lessened is,
Their sway of pendulum diminishes !

LXXXVIII.

Laws such as these eclipsed all past research,
    And astral revolution brought about;
The pupils of Pythagoras, the Church,
    On their discovery were put to rout.
The men of light could see "the promised land,"
But time for ent'ring it was not to hand!

LXXXIX.

'Tis from discoveries great, greater arise;
    And so it came about that on the road
Laid down by Kepler, Newton trod likewise:
    He gravitation's laws observed, the mode
Of falling bodies common to all mass,
The universal law, none can surpass!

XC.

'Twas from long-suffering incessant thought
    The uniform and all-pervading law
Was attainèd, and the mechanism brought
    To order, as to how the planets draw
All unsupported bodies to the ground,
At rates proportioned to the mass that's found.

XCI.

The law by which the apple falls to the earth
    Is one original as mass, and acts
Through universal space and time; its birth
    "Behind the veil" is hidden, but the facts
Point to its operation since the stars
Were made—rolled planets, such as Mars.

XCII.

'Twas through the moon the corner-stone was laid
   Of gravitation's temple! now 'twas found
That it obeyed the same law as the staid
   Orb that it gladdens, that it circles round—
The law that guides the apple in its fall
And sways all matter, whether great or small.

XCIII.

But not alone does gravitation act
   Through the sun's mass on Luna, but all worlds
Circling with satellites in space, react
   Upon each other's mass; which fact unfurls
The glory of the law in heaven's expanse,
Whose reign is order—cosmic sustenance!

XCIV.

Thus Jove to Earth pays court in wheeling round
   The centre of his motion, at first phase
Through his attractive power, and then 'tis found
   Luna disturbance suffers from his ways
Of coquetry—obeying a magnet great,
Each mass's orbit tends to deviate!

XCV.

The Queen of Night, in path at phase called "new,"
   Bows to the solar magnet's influence,
And suffers deviation slightly too;
   At glory "full" the Earth in consequence
Of such attraction also is withdrawn
From the great lamp that lights us, ere the dawn.

XCVI.

Then with the moon's rotation, when she nears
  While circling with her lord Apollo's might,
At perihelion, the great charioteer's
  Loadstone attracts her, hastens on her flight.
Diana's course is bent, allured, repelled,
Yet still by gravitation's grip upheld.

XCVII.

With these exceptions, like a faithful wife,
  Diana reigns with loyalty; her path
From "eccentricity" is free, that strife
  That comes of swerving from the track that hath
Been meted to her.   Though she often bows
To gods at other phase, she keeps her vows!

XCVIII.

So with a comet or a falling star;
  The law of gravitation rules the swoop
Of matter in ellipse, and wand'ring far
  Even for untold ages, each must stoop
To its decree!   The comet's tail obeys
The self-same law when nearing solar blaze.

XCIX.

When it approaches the great light of day,
  The comet's tail's behind the comet's mass;
When it's flown past Sol's furnace, all the gay
  And glowing tail's absorbed, new fused to pass
Before the comet now.   Such is the force
Of gravitation in the mass's course!

C.

'Tis to the revolution of the Earth
 The moon its monthly voyage owes ; its speed,
Its distance, rate, determined were at birth :
 Had it been twice the distance, when 'twas freed,
Hurled into space, its rate would then have been
But half that meted the nocturnal queen.

CI.

Off from the mother, Earth, the moon was cast
 In mystic ages gone ; the molten state
And awful orbit in the long, long past
 Suffered the planet's mass to deviate ;
The mighty fragment into space was hurled,
And rolled, as Luna to the parent-world.

CII.

Two forms of energy her mass engage,
 That given her by the Earth, when she cast out
Her offspring from her side as equipage ;
 The other due to orbit round about
The fairy planet !   Gravitation guides
The earth-moon system as it onward glides !

CIII.

But for a law identical, the tides
 Would not exist ; that which we call the "spring"
By lunar gravitation's caused, besides
 That of the sun ; less powerful forces bring
On what are called the shallow or the "neap,"
For here a semi-lune acts on the deep !

CIV.

The ebb and flow of tides is brought about
    Through energies two distant orbs within,
That stored up in the moon when cast without,
    And that of Earth's rotation—daily spin.
The greater force effecting tidal flow
Comes from the roll of planet here below!

CV.

The moon when hurled was like a cannon-ball;
    A force of separation was once lent
The mass adrift—a form that authors call
    " Repose of energy;" the active form that's spent
Comes from the store of Earth's diurnal swing:
'Tis this that keeps Diana in her ring!

CVI.

The rhythm of the earth-moon system rests
    On gravitation's constant government,
But for the perfect spin, each orb attests,
    Which prehistoric time its voyage lent.
Like to the cannon-ball, the moon would boom
Back to the plains of Earth, and find its doom!

CVII.

Such is a sketch of the great principle
    That regulates all matter, rules all space:
All atoms, granules, masses, to the pull
    Of gravitation yield—the human race
Is rooted to the Earth by the same law
That sways a feather, Neptune tends to draw.

CHAPTER IV.

CVIII.

'Tis from the study of the meteor's play
   That a solution of the astral laws
Is gleaned—a knowledge of the sun, the "Milky Way;"
   For bodies luminous all find their cause
In meteoric matter, fused, condensed,
Once on a time, before their roll commenced!

CIX.

But given thus our meteoric mass,
   Whence came the "world-stuff" forming it? Did
      chance
Weld atoms into masses—these to meteors pass?
   Were masses due to mystic atoms' dance?
No! Elements of mass were ages' haze,
Till churned, condensed, made matter by Sol's rays.

CX.

For Herschel says that mass was nebulous
   In the beginning, and that play of force
And motion's dance, but nought miraculous,
   Acting on mass, evolved the great world's course !
Atoms to atoms joined, then great cohered
Till globules grew to globes and worlds appeared.

CXI.

Then energy, first passive, took to flight,
   And motion gave the mass which came to roll
Upon its axis, ere the forms of light
   And heat from rolling issued from the whole ;
Then gravitation hastened to the scene,
And planets started in the planes serene !

CXII.

From giant masses down to flocculi,
   A law of concentration sways and draws
Matter together ; clusters that on high
   Are dimly seen by glass, bend to the laws
Of integration !   Inorganic groups,
Wand'ring at large, communion find in groups !

CXIII.

Like to the planet in its growing state,
   All floating matter, ere its motion goes,
Tends to cohere, and thus to integrate
   Another mass : 'tis thus the cluster grows
Ere it's condensed, cooled down, solidified
Into a spheroid, whirling in its pride.

CXIV.

Little beginnings up above take rise,
　As here below—arrive at mighty ends;
The brightest satellite that gems the skies
　Was once a cloud diffused, and dim to lens;
Then condensation charmed it into gas
Ere liquid it became, ere solid mass.

CXV.

So transformation slowly came about
　Through integration; molten lava shrank
Into the ponderable; then orbs rolled out
　Of blazing nebulæ, of varying rank:
The simple bodies held eccentric course,
When first expelled, ere yielding motion's force.

CXVI.

But for a medium's resisting power
　Acting on moving bodies, all would tend
To gravitation's centre, all would scour
　In parallel direction, space, all bend
Back to their source; the planets but preserve
Through forces round about their compound curve.

CXVII.

'Tis everywhere the same, the spiral form
　Follows on motion in organic life;
In floating bodies bubbles e'en conform
　To taking corkscrew shapes.   Nature is rife
With instances: stir but a tranquil lake,
And rings concentric its sereneness shake!

CXVIII.

So with the branches and the leaves of trees,
    Their grace and beauty to the curve is due;
The growing heart in circles by degrees,
    In layers too finds development; so true
Responsive to initial law is growth,
That flowers to bloom by other law are loth!

CXIX.

Beauty of form results from motion's dance
    In lines of least resistance; breadth and length
Follow the laws of growth; all things advance
    Hereby to maturation, find their strength:
The damsel's beauty and the rosebud's shape
In complex curves rejoice, like features ape!

CXX.

All motion's rhythmical that is decreed
    To play by rise and fall; no balanced scale
Adjusts conflicting force; in magic speed
    The troop of suns career, the planets sail;
An undulating dance that knows no pause
Sustains each planet's course, all stellar laws!

CXXI.

A dance that's rhythmical—poised to the planes
    Of masses' flight; no matter what the size
Or distance of the orb, the rate remains
    For ever fixed; planets afar off rise
And set obedient to initial law,
Stamped by a First Great Cause with ne'er a flaw.

CXXII.

First nebulous, all matter strove
　To find a centre ; rotatory flight
Thenceforth engaged it to on axis move ;
　The rhythm only followed from the might
Of forces twain—that of repulsive throw
Being met by one attractive down below !

CXXIII.

Rhythm of motion then's a compound thing,
　Resulting from the spin of solar chief,
Incessant, axial ; the elliptic swing
　Follows initial force—the roll in chief
Of blazing Sol.　Here cosmic motion gains
Its origin, as insight well explains.

CXXIV.

All nature pulsates to the rhythmic throb
　Of solar force !　Instance the steamer's screw—
The laws of mechanism cannot rob
　It of vibration, for the spin holds true :
So with the train that runs along the rail,
Whose tremor thrills, oft makes the timid quail !

CXXV.

Light's undulation and Aurora's waves
　Impress us with the like mysterious law ;
The flash electric in its speed behaves
　As uniformly as the bending straw
To the rude wind !　Motion's replete with power
To circles form—the planes of space to scour.

CXXVI.

The tear that tumbles on the infant's cheek,
   The ruby-tinted cell of vital stream,
The iridescent bow 'mid storm we seek,
   Partake of the round form ; such is the scheme
Of cosmic law ! And highest human art
The classic line of beauty seeks t' impart.

CXXVII.

So with the surface of the sea ; the waves,
   Compounded yet of smaller, rise and fall
In rhythmic curves ; the cannon-ball behaves
   In voyage just the same, though critical
Apparently in flight, for here the ellipse
Is faintly shadowed as the missile dips.

CXXVIII.

The ruling monarch of the spangled sky
   Enjoys eternal day, and freely turns
Upon his mighty axis, rhythmicly
   His spots revolve—traverse the mass that burns.
Sol rolls upon himself in spheral blaze
Once in the space of five-and-twenty days !

CXXIX.

The awful force exerted by the sun
   Acting through space, establishes the rhythm
Of revolution, drives on, once begun,
   The retinue of orbs, of stars, and with 'em
The troop of satellites ; the counter force
Of gravitation's neutralised, of course !

CXXX.

His yawning craters, shaped like willow-leaves,
   Open and close with blast volcanic; gales
Of rage magnetic reign; the monarch heaves,
   Ready to burst; eternally prevails
The storm! Some twenty thousand miles
Each spot encompass, fury mad beguiles!

CXXXI.

At first the nebula, intensely hot,
   Forming the solar system reached without
Beyond the plane of Neptune; now you've got
   A hazy notion how things came about,
If to the cloud you motion bring to bear,
And compound forces acting everywhere!

CXXXII.

Motion undoubtedly of mass must lead
   To some fixed form ere rhythm follows on,—
Be it a sphere or spheroid that is freed,
   It, too, must centre have to roll upon;
From motion's dance acting on seething mass
Forces will come, contraction, heat will pass!

CXXXIII.

Contraction's grip will make the ball to roll
   Faster and faster as the area's less
Of revolution; flattened at each pole
   The body will become, the weight compress
The bulging centre out, the equator's zone
Being sometimes freed and made to go alone!

CXXXIV.

The force repulsive greater once became
  Than that of gravity, and so a ring
Became detached from the evolving frame,
  To whirl in lower plane of space, to swing
In a new orbit: then unbalanced force
The ring continuous soon wrecked, of course !

CXXXV.

The fragments joined by gravity's fell strain
  Then grew rotund, and Sol's frame rolled around,
Tracking each other in the self-same plane—
  The larger hindered in the depths profound,
The smaller fragments' progress by their weight,
When aggregation settled each one's fall.

CXXXVI.

But to return to the dismembered mass ;
  Contraction, radiation, did not cease
Its contour to consolidate, amass
  Its parts component, till another piece
Was once more cast without from its tense side :
In short, a satellite in all its pride.

CXXXVII.

The magic revolution of the sun
  In mystic times primeval brought about
Alike catastrophes he'd once begun,
  Till family of orbs soon rolled without.
Thus fragments annular the planets framed
Through cosmic forces we've already named !

CXXXVIII.

In the beginning girdles then were cast
  From the diffused and glowing solar chief,
Which suffered rupture in abysses vast ;
  Then integration gained ; planets, in brief,
Were thus first formed ! So says the great Laplace,
Whose grand hypothesis none can surpass.

CXXXIX.

But work means friction, friction heat, and so
  This element in glowing rays, set free
Into the awful void so long ago,
  Made bodies all glow with ferocity.
The oblate spheres could only come about
Through limpid matter pressed on from without.

CXL.

Motion, when dissipated, gave out heat,
  And so to masses' integration led ;
The broken shell, dislodged, went to complete
  The growing planet's form, which shortly sped
On its established tour ; the complex dance
Of matter led to single now—by chance.

CXLI.

Cooling went on (contraction's grip, I mean),
  Which led to density—diminished size,
Ere the new orb serenely could careen
  Upon its axis : heat to exercise
Its glowing power continued without fail ;—
A force that must in growing orbs prevail.

CXLII.

Whether the motion followed from the crash
　　Of integrating matter or the flood
Of generated currents, would be rash
　　For us to speculate ; but this holds good,
That globes dropped into space revolved at least
With one proclivity from west to east.

CXLIII.

For all the planets and the satellites
　　Revolve around the sun in their career,
Excepting Uranus, whose plane invites
　　To independent roll to others near,
In planes concentric ;—thus is each globe cast
' Adaptively to Sol's ecliptic vast !

CXLIV.

The law of revolution is reversed
　　In Uranus and Neptune (?), from the fact
That the ancestral rings that tumbled first
　　Into these planes, when concentrating lacked
In mass the same oblateness as the rest ;
Which drove their satellites from east to west.

CXLV.

A fairy hooped-shaped pattern was their form,
　　Which collapsed into figure nearly round
When into space precipitated warm ;
　　Hence the rotation's at right angles found
To the ecliptic plane, or through each pole ;
This is why satellites reversely roll.

CXLVI.

The retinue of globes compactness gained,
    Each from the integration of a ring
Once cast off from the sun ; ere each attained
    An independent roll, each went to fling
Its rind to make the next—the molten peel
Varying from quoit to hoop shape in its reel !

CXLVII.

From Neptune on to Jove, the rings increased
    In their diameter, till Jove's vast frame
Well-nigh absorbed the compact mass ; at least
    Contracting, shed such thin rind as became
But asteroids.   Here concentration failed
An orb to make, through forces that prevailed.

CXLVIII.

Thus grew the planets !   The revolving mass
    Continuing to shrink, faster and faster whirled,
Till a fresh glowing ring began to pass
    From the orb cooling, which anon unfurled
Soon its own satellite—a startling view,
Which Saturn's present ring attests as true !

CXLIX.

Such is the nebular hypothesis
    Shadowed by Kant and sketched out by Laplace ;
And brilliant, fascinating view it is,
    Even to this day, which Proctor's can't surpass ;
It chimes with evolution's clearest sound,
And rings with reason's subtlest sense profound !

CL.

Truth is its goal, and Triumph is its hope,
    Patience its watchword, Wisdom is its crown,
Reverence its breastplate with the sons that grope
    After heavenly light, that so oft seems to frown.
Once the keys of nature hidden were from race;
Now the weary students see things face to face.

CHAPTER V.

CLI.

Time was, unchronicled, when the vast sea—
   The mystic empyrean—was opaque;
Diluted sunshine filled immensity
   Ere the great force unknown began to shake
The gaseous chaos with a magic wand,
Ere Sol became rotund, ere daylight dawned!

CLII.

The fluid haze with which things first began
   A gradual diminution underwent,
In vast circumference, in boundless span,
   As each ring tumbled into space, was spent
In fashioning a world—the central core
Retreating formed the sun, as said before.

CLIII.

No magic "*fiat*" started, ready made,
   The orbs and satellites, the stars that glow
In the celestial sea, in varying grade
   Of place, might, rhythm—but a process slow;
A growth of mist chaotic but explains
The birth of matter in the heavenly planes!

CLIV.

Though many earnest searchers in the quest
   Of how in heaven's expanse mass came to roll,
Have from a maze of thought emerged, expressed
   Their own pet theories—there's Mr. Croll,
Who thinks that blazing suns were simply formed
From motion's loss in heat when meteors " swarmed."

CLV.

In other words, that meteoric shoals,
   Whirling in mighty stream in far-off planes,
Collided, and set spinning through their poles
   A retinue of orbs ; the view explains
Nought as to how the glorious lamp of day
Keeps up its glowing heat, its constant ray !

CLVI.

The brilliant flare that kindled at the crash
   Of atoms must have temporary been,
Like to the fitful beacon light, the flash
   Of heaven's artillery, when in tempest seen ;
The fund of energy that's thus outpoured
A sun from such a means could not afford !

CLVII.

No theory like Laplace's can explain
   Why the sun's first-born planets were immense,
Or why those near his disc did small obtain—
   Facts that are purely physical ; or whence
Like contrasts governed all the satellites
Which first evolved, were mighty, then were mites !

F

CLVIII.

Think but of Saturn's orb to make it clear;
His mass leviathan nigh utilised
The excess of mist that fringed the solar sphere;
While, after Jove, the matter that sufficed
To younger planets frame was powerless quite
To build another orb of equal might!

CLIX.

The retinue of moons that once was cast
From Saturn's equatorial bulging zone
Had a like history; for the first were vast,
Such as Iapetus, Hyperion;
While the six moonlets that from off his side
Fell later on were miniature beside.

CLX.

And further testimony helps the view,
Such as the yearly outpour from the sun
In heat—a fact that's to contraction due,
Such as the retreating since the great year One
Of the fire-king, whose mass falls in, in space
Four miles a century from the human race!

CLXI.

Now, Proctor says the planets simply grew
"Through meteoric indraughts" in each plane
About the sun—the "meteoric view,"
When gravitation welded with its strain
And grip the mass; that planets near the sun
Went through this process slowly, every one!

CLXII.

Through their velocity the meteors vast
  Quick aggregation found, and hence the globes
Nearest the sun "ran small," though others cast
  Out of the "nick of time" forsook the robes
Of the orb forming.   Here repulsive might
Hurled the stray body as it came in sight !

CLXIII.

His view sets forth, too, that the greatest crash
  Of meteors took place in the plane of Jove
Where mass abounded—slower the rush
  Of matter here, and less inclined to move !
Into the vortex hence were meteors thrown
Pell-mell, for Jupiter's vast bulk to own !

CLXIV.

Matter adrift found union up to Earth
  In rapid rhythmic roll, when meteor's store
Faltered awhile—to asteroids gave birth !
  For forces twain of Jove and Sol now bore
Opposing strain upon the evolving mass,
And baulked the planet "building" here, alas !

CLXV.

Which brings us to the glorious girdled orb
  Called Saturn, with his tinted surface gay :
Here is a planet destined to absorb
  All other worlds in interest, by the way
His globe is poised within encircling belt
Of mystic meteors tending all to melt !

CLXVI.

His belt has riveted, and still beguiles,
    The loftiest intellects that upwards soar,
Being quite in span three hundred thousand miles,
    Which nought of depth includes—two hundred o'er.
The rings—composed of tiny satellites—
When analysed, are meteors by rights !

CLXVII.

Each mite's attracted by the other's power,
    And all by that of Saturn ; each one moves
In its appointed plane—the mighty shower
    Answering the mass with rhythm, Maxwell proves :
The granules order keep with globe that reels,
Like rings revolving round the spokes of wheels.

CLXVIII.

For his control, all active forces, known
    To hedge his path, must weighed have been in scales
Of intellect, or he had ne'er alone
    Resisted all those fierce cyclonic gales
That rage around ; by Wisdom, and not Force,
Has Saturn governed his mysterious course !

CLXIX.

The revolution of the Saturnian ring
    Is brought about through force centrifugal
Of planetary bulk, whose rhythmic swing
    Controls, in constant wavelets magical,
Its perfect orbit ; compensating strain
Of moons attendant keeps it in its plane.

CLXX.

Composed of meteors in the form of dust,
  Friction, collision, follows on the play
Of neighbouring particles which strive to thrust
  Each from the other's place; the brilliant spray
Of the mysterious ring is thus explained;
'Tis to the glowing lava o'er it rained!

CLXXI.

The whirling planet keeps within its ring,
  By gravitation's equipoise; the belt
Of myriad meteors formed, being forced to swing
  With rhythm in its plane, as round they pelt:
The retinue of moons the orb enjoys
Steadies the globe, adjusts its equipoise!

CLXXII.

Cohesion keeps the particles in place,
  Although they travel round at different speed
From that at which the ring keeps up its pace,
  Which rolls distinct from orb, though never freed!
The pliant globe in chief the system sways
And keeps intact the belt in which it plays!

CLXXIII.

Ring of enchantment! what will be thy fate?
  Will Saturn cast thee off? or will thy grace
A dissolution find in ages late?
  Or wilt thou go to form in future race
Another planet, leaving Saturn free
To whirl unfettered in immensity?

CLXXIV.

Thy history shows thou formerly wert thrust
   From off thy planet's mass through rival powers
Will then thy mighty form suck in the dust
   Of matter nebulous once cast in showers
From off thy seething frame?   Thine inner ring
Most clearly points to some such reasoning!

CLXXV.

Wheel within wheel, the giant girdle swings
   Like a resplendent bow around the mass,
Whose halo is composed of several rings,
   Teeming with meteors glowing as with gas:
The nearest meteoric ring in shape,
Through its transparency, resembles crape!

CLXXVI.

Unsuited for the abode of living things,
   What useful office does this planet serve?
Does he reflect the light Apollo brings,
   Give warmth to satellites around, preserve
Set forms of life thereon? or does he reign
To glory shed us men within his plane?

CLXXVII.

Whether the giant hoop will find its doom
   In loss atomic, frictional decay,
Or be *en masse* hurled swiftly to the gloom
   Of an unplumbed immensity one day,
Is now conjecture!   But the "files of time"
Point to the wreck of Saturn's ring sublime!

CLXXVIII.

The ring, still nebulous, that typifies
   And girdles this expansive mystic globe,
Lends the most signal proof within the skies
   Of cosmic evolution !   Speaking robe
Of splendour ! meteoric crown of grace !
Bewitching halo, grandest decking space !

CLXXIX.

The theory of Design quite fails t' explain
   Why, if unpeopled, hosts of satellites
Do other planets deck in heaven's domain,
   Although 'tis argued that they shine as lights
To glad the creatures there with nightly glow,
When Sol has gone to shine in planes below !

CLXXX.

But granted other worlds are peopled thus,
   We reason fail t' obtain from such a view
Why Saturn's largest lamps do farthest reach ;
   Or why that Uranus has moons so few,
Seeing that from the sun he's twice as far
As that bright neighbour, the Saturnian star !

CLXXXI.

And so with Neptune, we are baffled quite
   To fact explain why but a single moon
Has he, thus far removed in dead of night,
   Unless his swift roll compensates for boon
Of further retinue—unless his veil
In light rejoices that we cannot scale !

CLXXXII.

The laws of Time and Space, alone, will throw
　　Light on these riddles, as they tell the roll
Of all the orbs, though man presumes to know,
　　Before "the veil's" withdrawn, ere nature's soul
Yields to the "telic" lens. The spectral beam
Will one day tell us what now mysteries seem!

CLXXXIII.

Just as the law of gravitation finds
　　A place within the cloisters of our creed,
So, later, evolution, in the minds
　　Of truth-inquiring lovers, will take seed;
For both are laws of Time and Space, their dower
Methods divine and principles of power.

CLXXXIV.

The age will come when all will have to bow
　　To the Time-ruler, spite of bitterness!
The law which tells us how worlds grow, and how
　　They're growing still—the greater and the less:
Magic creation will be laid aside,
And faith in Evolution have full-tide!

CHAPTER VI.

CLXXXV.

Age after age the peopled planet ploughs
   Her journey through the unfenced fields of space,
·And yet, the meteoric hail, her bows
   Assails in thousands—her benignant face;
The stream of tiny stars that gem the skies ·
Pervade the void like microscopic flies!

CLXXXVI.

Evolved from nebulæ in æons gone,
   Or hurled out from the roar of growing sun,
What useful purpose do these missiles vast
   Subserve? Do they contribute, every one,
Appointed meed of duty to each earth,
By lending atoms, integrating girth?

CLXXXVII.

With fury quite tempestuous they hail
   On to the coasts of whirling spheres around,
Jostling with ether, wrecking in their trail
   Matter and motion, everywhere around
Being pulverised! Their mission seems to be
To planets feed, meet Sol's insolvency!

CLXXXVIII.

The balance at his bank of energy
　　Must be maintained, matter Sol cannot lack,
And what he gives in force, velocity,
　　To kindle paths of beauty, he takes back
In meteoric kind!　Attractive power
Brings to his bosom myriads every hour!

CLXXXIX.

So that Apollo's energies proceed
　　In part from meteors hailed upon his disc,
Though 'twould be rash to state they solely feed
　　The King of Time and Space, as down they whisk.
The capital, derived from solar planes
By force magnetic, all the rest explains!

CXC.

The light of day, the very pulse of life,
　　The power of winds and storms, the engine's pant,
Matter's career, and motion's dance, the strife
　　Of gale Atlantean, are significant
Of energies once pent up in the shell
Of flying matter ere it, sunwards, fell.

CXCI.

From the august and molten monarch came
　　The birth of force that gave the meteors flight:
Hence banished once, they now refeed the flame
　　Of solar mass, by giving up the might
Of their velocity!　Augmented store
Of power comes from the flight the meteor bore!

CXCII.

In distance then, the element of scale,
   Lies the chief secret of the source from whence
The solar system draws its stores!   The hail
   Of meteors from the vast circumference
Of space, the thousand forms of might,
Sol's vast attraction gathers in by right !

CXCIII.

Just as the snowball, growing in its roll,
   Volume and mass begets as on it speeds,
So the great lamp of day acquires the whole
   Of his resources, his material needs !
Passing through regions rich in stones of space,
He, meteoric shoals draws in apace !

CXCIV.

Phœbus, the Fairy-world, and planets all
   In constitution elementary
Are just the same ; for meteors both fall
   And reign upon their bodies constantly :
This latter fact explains how planets grew,
Are growing still—the " meteoric view."

CXCV.

The varying rings eccentric that comprise
   The orbits of the meteoric realm,
Their tour ubiquitous within the skies,
   Tend earnest thinkers quite to overwhelm
As to the law of matter ; for no plane
Has been found out that lacks the meteor's reign !

CXCVI.

The telescopic view of planets gay
  Suggests that they, in order, were evolved
From the sun outwards—not the other way,
  As that called "nebular" would have them rolled,
But each one settled down in order meet
For final roll as rushed the meteors fleet!

CXCVII.

The meteoric origin of globes
  Is shadowed forth then by the general play
Of matter—meteors forming all the robes
  Of circling worlds; though facts the other way—
The mystery of Saturn's ring and Jove,
Are not herein explained—how matter strove!

CXCVIII.

Now Sol's corona, zodiacal light,
  His dazzling brilliance come of candent beams
Of meteoric hail, the whirl, the flight
  Of glowing atoms: planetary scenes
Abound in echo of the oft-told tale,
The wealth of meteors that around prevail!

CXCIX.

Though why the other planets do not swing
  Within a girdle reaching far and wide,
Since they evolvèd were from centre-ing
  Of meteors diffuse, we can't decide!
Set forms of force in latitudes must reign,
And plastic matter mould becoming plane!

CC.

Why elements chaotic should have gained
  The laws of integration, motion's charm,
The pulse of order, cannot be explained ;
  Whether they came from nebulæ or swarm
Of meteoric mass !   But that they sprung
With purpose wise " to order " must be sung !

CCI.

Persistence of the Force that reigns supreme
  O'er matter must an origin have had,
A law of distribution, or the stream
  Of circling worlds, of stars, had not been clad
With beauty, motion definite !   Some Will
Started the cosmos, and controls it still.

CCII.

Whether the Universe eternally reigned,
  Or was evolved from simple plastic haze !
Its orderly control must have obtained
  An influence from without, or else the blaze
Of solar beams adapted had not been
To planets' weal, or stellar planes serene !

CCIII.

'Tis in the tropics that the flashing sparks,
  That vanish in the vault of heaven, shine out
In greatest brilliancy ! which, Burns remarks,
  Comes from the purity of air, no doubt !
Here shooting stars more often glad the eye,
Like rocket's dart, illuminate the sky.

CCIV.

The boundless pure cerulean tint welled forth
 In heaven's expanse reflects the meteor's hues
With greater clarity than in the north,
 Whether the fleeting star be red or blue ;
Pale, faint, and yellow lights here dart and die,
And ceaselessly to heaven's wealth testify.

CCV.

Sometimes impulsive is the meteor's flight ;
 Repulsion wrecks the mass as on it goes,
Giving each atom hurled a track of light ;
 The mass contracting then, no longer glows,
Till once more swelling out to burst again,
It tricks its beams with glory in new plane.

CCVI.

Though order certainly is heaven's first law,
 Wielding the meteor's flight ; although the spray
We see, our ancestors in wonder saw,
 Results from intermission on its way
Of force repulsive as these bodies fly :
We thus explain their flash, plunge, destiny !

CCVII.

The height at which the meteor is found
 Seems to be fixed at four-and-seventy miles,
That is, when human eye its headlong bound
 Observes with wonder from the British Isles :
The brilliant arc of light is lost to view
After a tour of miles—some twenty-two !

CCVIII.

The speed at which the falling star careers
   Is twice as great as that with which the Earth
Rolls round the sun !—her annual journey steers ;
   So that the force inherent at its birth
Must have been drawn from out the depths of space
By solar pull, or hurled forth from Sol's face.

CCIX.

Matter is fused when travelling at the rate
   Of thirty miles a second, and the crust,
Being liquefied, at once assumes the state
   Of scintillating cloud, of glittering dust ;
The most refractory mass that wings the plane
Is thus reduced, soon casts behind its train.

CCX.

The fleeting starlets tailed that gem the sky
   And intersect our orb are "falling stars ;"
The balls which strike th' Earth's veil we dignify
   With name of "meteor ;" while the little bars
That, cooling, strike this globe, are styled by rights
Neither of these, but simply "aërolites."

CCXI.

When in the crucible of spectral light
   The visitor of space is analysed,
A yellow band, though sometimes yellow-white,
   Reveals its nature—for so long disguised,
The iridescent glow that marks its flight
To nothing points but soda-flame by night !

CCXII.

Though spectral bands pointing to other kinds
    Of matter earthy, such as phosphorus,
Potassium, are seen, so the great minds
    In principles hold forth we can't discuss !
What photographic art, the telescope,
Fails to detect, comes from the spectroscope !

CCXIII.

Man's nature hates all mystery, it must
    Fathom the secrets of all cosmic laws ;
And so it comes about the meteor's thrust
    Into the tube of light—to yield the cause
Of its career, its properties, the might
The body gathered in the dead of night !

CCXIV.

The states that reign above are first obeyed :
    A vacuum within the distal end
Of a light-searcher starts on the crusade,
    Or the "first act," when heat comes to befriend
The subtle process : next, a feeble glow
Of light electric heats it from below !

CCXV.

"Act two : "—Heat tempered to a gentle glow
    Now plays upon the meteor in its cell,
And tint produces, when electric flow
    Is brought to bear upon the heavenly shell ;
The gas called "hydrogen" now meets the view,
And paints the spectrum with its dazzling hue !

CCXVI.

But particles from heaven have yet to yield
　　Still further secrets ; so a further charge
Of light electric's turned upon the field
　　Of observation, when in volumes large
Compounds of carbon limn upon the plate
Their bands of beauty—as precipitate !

CCXVII.

And other properties alike proceed
　　From matter wrecked, upon the plane below ;
When force caloric's pushed and made to feed
　　The field of scrutiny, we get the glow
Of primal element as met on Earth,
The gas magnesium springing into birth.

CCXVIII.

And other spectra—all of varying hue—
　　Play on the prism of the instrument,
Which first collects, then breaks the rays in two
　　Ere it transmits through chamber (that is bent)
The elemental bands ; sometimes a red,
Then violet, yellow line on screen is shed !

CCXIX.

Flutings of carbon bright point to the glow
　　Of mass reduced, then bands of emerald green
Reveal magnesia's base, though rendered now
　　Into a gas : with greatest heat, there's seen
The metal iron—such properties in chief
Compose the meteor when reduced in brief !

G

CCXX.

The great philosopher, Lucretius,
   Taught that the atoms tossed in times gone by
And dashed in space with gale tempestuous,
   Until at last their whirl within the sky
Acquired an orbit—that eccentric flight
Came from the attractive influence of Sol's might.

CCXXI.

The unwearying atoms course around in zones
   The solar plane once drawn from the profound
Of sunless gloom ; the meteoric stones
   Then gain attractive and repulsive bound :
Collision follows from the Earth's bright face
Being pelted by the missiles in their race.

CCXXII.

Like a balloon drifting in gale of snow,
   This orb her journey steers, heedless of storm
Of falling bodies, and of hurtling blow
   Of atoms on the wing and multiform ;
The planet's face sometimes exceeds, then falls
Below the speed of restless meteor-balls.

CCXXIII.

Infinity of space is occupied
   With meteoric troops in every plane,
Spite of the mighty shoals solidified
   By aggregation into orbs that reign
In heaven's expanse, spite of the clusters spent
In evolution of the firmament.

STELLAR SONGS.

CCXXIV.

Like grains of sand upon the shingly shore
   Encroached upon by Herculean pull
Of inward tidal wave, the meteor
   Holds out in wealth, is just as plentiful ;
Though fifteen million grains fall on the earth
Of matter in a day, there's still no dearth.

CCXXV.

Which nought includes of yearly August fall
   Of continental growth, whose orbit's range
Extends from solar plane to Neptune's power ;
   Nor of the gay " Leonides," whose strange
Eccentric tour to Uranus enthralls
Mankind more keenly than all scattered balls !

CCXXVI.

Systems of settled roll, and wondrous planes
   Revealing in their tours the heritage
Of most prodigious forms, the bold campaigns
   That farthest, deepest, darkest depths engage
Of space, are all excluded here, I say,
From meteoric clouds that feed Sol's ray !

CCXXVII.

The planes in which systems untold engage
   Their cycles of activity extend
From path coincident of solar rage
   To every angle with it—forwards bend
E'en to coincidence again, though now
Systems their journeys backwards have to plough !

CCXXVIII.

The yawning gulf of the eternal void
  Is tenanted, beyond Sol's equipage,
With wealth of meteors tending asteroid,
  And star and world that telescope can't gauge
The number of!   A rhythmic flight of mites
Decks unknown centres, unnamed satellites!

CCXXIX.

Though the attractive force of earthy orb
  To entangle in her envelope the stray
Outlying troops is feeble, to absorb
  By gravitation's grip the distant sway
Of pageants that attend on other planes,
Yet here the ruling orb their mass constrains.

CCXXX.

Earth's roll, together with the flight of mass,
  Makes matter aggregate at large in space
From minor systems, but does not amass
  Her wealth by the attraction to her face
Of distant clusters, that in settled course
Bow to the rule of other planets' force.

CCXXXI.

Though many of the shoals that represent
  The fleeting systems as they near the sun
Are drawn into the furnace, quickly spent,
  The greater number swing in plane begun
Eternally, though columns that embrace
The sun this year, have vanished next in space.

CCXXXII.

On to the Hades of abyssmal space,
　To spend the winter of their restless tour,
The giant shoals pursue their path, their pace
　Of wild ellipse, of ebon temperature ;
The brilliant meteoric ocean meets
Small opposition to its stately fleets.

CCXXXIII.

Abounding thus within the planes of space,
　What is the origin of falling stars ?
Do writhing mounds, volcanic from their base,
　Endow them like the thunderbolts of Mars
With their velocity ?　Or did the moon
Once cast them from her side one afternoon ?

CCXXXIV.

They travel from the depths of space ; the voids
　No glass can reach, as other bodies round
About the sun career, like asteroids
　In groups and cycles run, and e'er abound :
Their long ellipses tend them all to roam
Through every plane until they wander home.

CCXXXV.

Nothing above differs from that below
　In composition ; all the metals, mass,
The vapour incandescent in its glow,
　That issues from the meteor, can't surpass
The properties of Earth ; one common source
Gives birth to matter !　'Tis a solar force !

CCXXXVI.

Whether the solar system known to men
　　Cast out the meteors, sent them on their tour
Like floating clouds of waifs, is more than pen
　　Can say for certain; this alone is sure,
Like to the short-lived comets, they all run
In planes determined by some distant sun!

CCXXXVII.

Whether they come from solar craters, face
　　Of unknown suns, from fierce cyclonic throes
Of dying worlds, or from the depths of space,
　　Their wealth above's the same, and undergoes
But little change, though through them worlds and planes
Are built, being built up, still no dearth remains!

CCXXXVIII.

All parts of space through which the Earth careers
　　Abound in meteoric flocculi;
Some thirty thousand strangers, it appears,
　　Pelt the revolving planet in the sky
Eternally!　No wonder that the girth
Of whirling planets grows—such as the Earth!

CCXXXIX.

Comets are nothing more than clustered shoals
　　Of meteors, all drifting in a cloud,
Whose dire collision heats them like to coals
　　Burning with whitest heat!　Such is their crowd!
The brilliant "star-like point" that rules the mass
Of light reflecting sparks is nought but gas!

CCXL.

A haze of lustrous atoms decks the head,
  The dazzling centre, from which oft a ray—
A lurid flame of fire—is often shed :
  Such was Donati's apparition gay.
The light welled forth comes from the head's own blaze
Which rules the tail, shining with borrowed rays !

CCXLI.

The wealth holds on, the vault of heaven abounds
  In kindred species of illumined grains
As beautifully disposed in compact mounds :
  Such are the nebulæ with floating manes
Of shattered matter !   These, when analysed,
Are nought but meteors volatilised !

CCXLII.

The very light that lingers round their place
  In the eternal void comes from the play,
The assaults of meteors booming on their face ;
  So with the glory of the " Milky Way,"
The phosphorescent glow that marks its site
Is mostly due to meteors in their flight !

CCXLIII.

Arrest of motion, dissipated heat,
  Proceeding from the wreck of waifs and strays,
Explains the glitter of the curious fleet
  Of drifting swarms, of meteor-laden haze :
Bombardment sets on fire the vaporous girth
Of nebulæ ! reflects the glow to Earth !

CCXLIV.

All giant clusters in the ethereal sea
   Have an attractive influence on mass
Sweeping without; 'tis thus apparently
   Bodies are utilised and turned to gas!
Thus worlds become evolved, and realms of wealth
Through floating matter being caught up by stealth!

CCXLV.

Systems and suns from diverse forms arise
   Of gaseous torrents, tending all to cool
Ere they yield up their glory in the skies,
   Of elemental shape! Such is the rule,
The Reign of Law! comets and nebulæ
Alike conform, acquire sphericity!

CCXLVI.

The elongated cluster with its glow
   Star-laden in Andromeda, that gem,
The keyhole constellation in Argo,
   Orion's "arrow-pointed" diadem,
The "crab," the "dumb-bell" patterns that adorn
The skies, will shine as stars some future morn!

CCXLVII.

But mass, that's nebulous, must undergo
   Consolidation's grip, ordeal of heat,
Of flame that's simply furious in its flow,
   Ere the new stellar object's made complete;
The blazing body with its vaporous robe
Must be cooled down ere it's a perfect globe!

CCXLVIII.

Cooling's an attribute of suns and stars,
 The satellites of planets, nebulæ,
Ere reaching spheral glory—such as Mars,
 And motion that's defined in heavenly sea,
For Tellus once was but a little sun
That cooling underwent ere life begun !

CCXLIX.

A wave of heat, that passes from the spray
 Of cometary atoms to the forge
Of solar continent, describes the play
 Of all celestial bodies that disgorge
Their vapours out, down to the planes of cold
The satellites of Earth and Sirius bold.

CCL.

So say the pictures speaking of the rays
 Limned by the hosts of heaven, the brightest hues
Pointing to comets, meteoric haze :
 While fainter bands come from the solar mines,
A law of condensation rules the rate,
The play of light bands on the " spectral plate " !

CCLI.

Stages of evolution mark the growth
 Of dawning worlds, of finished hemispheres ;
A law of progress rules matter above—that loath
 To arrive at spheral beauty, perfect spheres
And worlds worn out ; for dissolution reigns,
Like evolution, in the heavenly planes !

CCLII.

Though dust that's meteoric goes to mould
   By aggregation all the hosts of heaven,
Comets and nebulæ and stars, we're told,
   Ere generated heat conspires to leaven,
To evolve the growing mass: eddies of force
Then start the shining bodies on their course!

CCLIII.

Such is the part which meteors play in space,
   In building worlds, in aggregating mass
Through atoms concentrating in set place
   And being swayed by motion! They surpass
Hereby all elements in kindling and
Evolving worlds—as now we understand!

CHAPTER VII.

CCLIV.

WE therefore see the universe of haze
  Having evolved the mirrors that abound—
Still-lights and twinkling, those of feeblest rays
  Within the vault of heaven—to the profound
Scattered pell-mell, as meteors into space
The useless dust that failed an orb to grace !

CCLV.

How came the stately sequence of events
  We've here revealed ?   Has wandering matter power
Inherent to change form, show motion ?   Whence
  Came the weird force that flower after flower
Of heaven evolved ?   Did timely, lucky chance
Give pulse to matter, make its atoms dance ?

CCLVI.

Is "world-stuff" infinite—having no end
  And no beginning, constant in quantity,
Changing alone in form, with power to spend
  Itself in chemic force, or gravity ?
Or is't past finding out, the living robe
  Of an almighty power, that framed each globe ?

CCLVII.

If we contend that force is motion's mode,
    An outcome of a primal restless mass,
We get no farther than it's first abode,
    In ferment nebulous, chaotic gas:
We only find therein a medium
For matter, don't its origin o'ercome!

CCLVIII.

All verbal definition seems to fail
    T' express the origin of force—that power,
That "ultimate idea"—"behind the veil,"
    Having extension!   Universal dower!
Ethereal essence!   What we all must feel
Is, that 'tis Nature's pulse—scaled with a seal!

CCLIX.

The force that once carved out the living world,
    That formed, reformed, evolved the universe,
That, from a nebula, systems unfurled,
    Whose light is immortality—the nurse
Of worlds still growing! that fails us to discuss
The "all" of Nature—the mysterious!

CCLX.

But to its attributes!   Is force endowed
    For all time *ab initio* by some Will
That's ever in His works, that speaks aloud
    Through His created children, yet is still
In essence past discovery? whose cause
Sustains, develops all the cosmic laws?

CCLXI.

Is universal order but a mode
   Of thought divine?   Are Nature's forces nought
But forms of energy within—the abode
   Of power divisible?   Or is there aught
In matter's frame sufficient for the play
   Of all the forms of life we see to-day?

CCLXII.

But some one answers me : "Such is a view
   Of Immanence in Nature—Godhead thinned
Down to a pantheistic creed, in lieu
   Of one that's personal.   Cast to the wind
Such an idea !   To all-pervading Force
Beings of reason couldn't have recourse !"

CCLXIII.

As well assert, "An artist's finished work
   Rests in his canvas, is embodied there
His mind, himself !"   Both cannot therein lurk ;
   Though pigment is the means of beauty rare !
Volition must explain creation's dye,
And typify a Personality !

CCLXIV.

That vast Intelligence, Perception, Thought,
   Should mould the play of force, from matter spring,
Is beyond reason ; but that worlds were wrought
   By mind beyond matter's quite another thing !
If matter's pregnant with all Natural laws,
We surely must dismiss a First Great Cause !

CCLXV.

Yet nought of genius, no heroic deed,
    No feat of arms, is e'er performed below,
That man an authorship does not accede,
    Honour and adulation too bestow :
Then why do mortals wilfully deny
Supremacy of mind to One on high?

CCLXVI.

When we behold the magic complex loom,
    Its wondrous mechanism in full play,
Weaving the cotton in the carding-room,
    Spinning the threadlets there, across the way
Sending the shuttle—making " weft and woof "—
As to the " whence " of all we need no proof!

CCLXVII.

Though our eyes light upon mechanic acts,
    Lever's reactions, rolling pulse of wheels,
Adaptive motion to an axis—facts
    And details hundredfold, which sight reveals ;
We know a motive-power—which " force " we call—
Lingers unseen, yet works " behind a wall " !

CCLXVIII.

Invention's child alone plays on this side,
    Obeying the parent " man," whose subtle craft
Controls the finished product ! Time and tide
    Direct the engineer, who guides the shaft.
Though automatic acts within it rise,
A hidden power decides its energies.

CCLXIX.

So is't with Nature; there's another side
  To forces navigate "behind the veil;"
Her powers within are impotent to guide
  The music of the spheres, can't her avail!
The cosmic engine but obeys the helm
Of mind that's hidden in a starry realm.

CCLXX.

He who hath both Intelligence and Will
  Must postulate as the Great Architect!
Varied design and beauty, that space fill,
  Cannot proceed from matter; we reject
Unfolding operations free from Thought!
Cosmos from Chaos *couldn't* thus be wrought!

CCLXXI.

Then let us, dowered with Reason, Thought, and Will,
  With reverence, as in a sacred shrine—
As we survey the wonders that heaven fill—
  Him homage pay that made the stars to shine!
For He can add new glories to new worlds,
And fresh creations limn, as each unfurls!

PART II.

Sonnets.

H

SONNETS.

—✦—

ON A POET: I. DEFINITION.

WHAT is a Poet?   Is it one who sings
   Songs of enchantment in an easy flow
   Teeming with passion, feeling? or who beau
Ideal of fancy paints, or fiction brings
To harmony of sound, whose minstrel wings
   Seek heaven's dome?   No!   Such is not a bard,
   But he who in chaste tongue can guard
The temple of the Muse, whose language rings
   Like music to the ear, the mind; who pearls
Of thought to mint of utterance has given
Attuned to Orphic lyre, whose pen has striven
   To finely touch our souls, whose song unfurls
The realm of beauty from truth's eminence;
He is a poet in the highest sense.

ON A POET: II. DEFINITION.

YES! he the sacred fire enshrines, the flash
  Of genius, who thought and feeling gives
  In rounded numbers smooth, who lives
To elevate man's being 'mid the clash
Of mental toils—the hurtling for that cash
  Men struggle for, who fancy in fine flowers
  Or fact sets in a garland, taste o'erpowers
For thoughts unworthy of the Muse or trash
Of vulgar sentiment; who beauty shows
  In Nature's mystic realm, in twinkling stars,
    In woman's grace, her voice, her sweetness too,
Her lustrous eye, her love—so pure; the rose
  In all its beauty; he who gates unbars
    Of eloquence in song's a poet true!

IMAGINATION : ITS CHARM.

IMAGINATION is the mint where dwells
   The soul of music, poetry, and love,
   Religion and the fine arts, all that move
Man's better nature ; 'tis that which dispels
Our gloom and purifies our sense ; from its deep wells
   We conjure up the spirits of romance,
   And revel while they rollick, sing, and dance ;
Its wealth our trouble soothes, our discord quells.

In the great realm of fiction its best coins
   Are struck, and circulate with force more real
Than sober reason's ; its best form enjoins
   Our highest culture, for it makes us feel
Like to the poet in his sacred den,
Where fresh creations wait upon his pen !

IMAGINATION : ITS SCOPE.

'Tis that which clothes our life with sentiment,
   Which floods with wonder things of sight and sound,
   And new creations limns—men to astound !
Moves us to tears, to smiles, to merriment ;
The arts inventive in its cause are spent ;
   Its varied children hold as by a spell
   Our spirits ; as in " Lear," when we dwell
On the great master's flight—magnificent !
Anacreon's song inflames as much as wine
   Youth's pulse ; so with a traveller's sketch, each gives
A meed of joy.   Our thoughts on the divine,
   The instinct of the simplest thing that lives,
Are no less real because we can't define
Their hidden modes of sense—their souls, in fine.

IMAGINATION : ITS SEAT.

WITHIN a field of cells that fringe the brain,
   Where fresh creations, old impressions spring,
   She holds her court, for ever ministering
To her lord, Reason—proudest Sovereign !
Love, Feeling, all the passions form her train,
   And Will transmits her message : whispers fleet
   With lightning wings on lines of silk compete
Her dreams to perfect, harmonise in plane
Of subtler sense.   Like the unsettled sea,
   Her ripples grow to waves, and then flow on
To order's ocean, though strange reefs their free
   Current of sailing final shore upon
Oft hinder—alien winds and tides
Ere Fancy's bark to Beauty's harbour glides !

IMAGINATION: ITS REALITY.

IMAGINATION's bounded by no shore,
  Though claiming the ideal for its realm;
  It is a play of thought, whose waves o'erwhelm
The universe of mind—flow on with store
Of wondrous freshness—ever more and more.
  It is an index of the soul unseen,
  That often points to truth that might have been;
'Tis Fancy's genius at Reason's door!
Great Shakespeare's Ariel is no less a charm,
  Nor scent of violet a fragrance sweet;
The carols of the birds that our hearts warm
  Are none the less realities though fleet,
The artist's gems on canvas no less real
Because their beauty fingers cannot feel.

LOVE: ITS NATURE.

You ask me what is love?　That subtle sense,
　That like a magnet towards all we conceive,
　Or hope, or fear, our bosom tempts to heave!
Love is imagination's fire intense,
With feeling mutual for that spirit hence
　That 'waits our own; the longing for those beams
　That kindle our eye's fancy, haunt our dreams;
The lips that fervour spell, lisp confidence;
The quest of portrait of our other self
　Is love's commission, spell, in the world's fight;
　Twin-soul, that shade will cast of all that's bright
And pure about us, scatter off the delf
　Of daily duty—whose heart *can* vibrate
　To our best feelings, harmonise our fate!

LOVE: ITS EMPIRE.

'Tis love that draws the infant to the font
   Of Nature's well, the stream that floats the bark
   Of childhood on life's eddies; 'tis the spark
That lights those throes of fancy wild which haunt
The breast of youth while bashful, giddy, gaunt;
   Love is the silken chain, the linken knot,
   Which heart to heart can bind and sever not;
'Tis manhood's guide that only true men vaunt;
The loadstone that attracts to grace of mould
   And loveliness of mind and character:
'Twas love's romance Leander took of old
   Across the Hellespont, to break to her
His troth, his Hero, what was passion's rage;
The constant beacon 'tis of every age!

LOVE : ITS INFLUENCE.

LOVE is the flame that burns within the breast,
  And penetrates our being with a glow
  Of rhapsody, that cheers us as we go
On life's highway, that lights with interest
The details of the road from east to west.
  Poets have tried to fathom it in vain ;
  It is the passion reason can't explain,
Though oft its slave—a willing lord at best !

Like the cathedral spire that holds aloft
  In graceful symmetry its golden cross,
As sign of sacredness, so love may oft
  Be likened ! as its heavenly light across
Our being shines ! 'Tis Cupid's talisman,
The Queen of Graces ruling human span !

LOVE: ITS SPELL.

YES! Love's the touch that makes the whole world kin,
   The rod of divination that hangs round
   Life's little span; in tent, hall, grove 'tis found,
The humblest hearth's its home; it lurks within
The cottage and the mansion; frees from din
   Of discord, unit, tribe; welds families
   In peace together; holds communities
In concord—social welfare rests herein!

Its sweet response is music to the one
   Who in its cause enlists; its silent note
Is sweeter than the sound of lyre; the sun
   No warmer rays or sunshine can promote.
Its reign of glory here is but a phase
Of higher love, which links itself with praise!

PATHOS.

No trait in human nature points to soul
  Like pathos; 'tis the key the heart unlocks
  Through the ward mercy 'mid fell worldly shocks,
The gentle Ariel bringing peace 'mid roll
Of earthly clouds; 'twas felt in Abram's dole
  At burning pile, in Desdemona's fate,
  In Gordon's when the English came "too late."
The kiss 'mid fiery drift that Paolo once stole
From his Francesca showed it; Rosamund
  The Fair claimed pathos when she took the cup
    Of poison from Queen Eleanor in bower;
And Newcome—prince of chivalry—swelled the fund!
  With Mary Queen of Scots when they gave up
    Their lives! 'Tis pity's brief; curb not its power!

THE AGE OF CHIVALRY.

There was a time when woman was enthroned
 A goddess in the temple of mankind,
 Madonna sanctified, spotless in mind,
Guarded by knighthood true; but now disowned
Is chivalry; customs polite are toned
 To rites of sense, not soul!   No Quixote's found,
 Or modern Sancho kneeling on the ground
Before his queen; obeisance is dethroned!
Arthurian knight-errant's seen no more
 At feet of Elaine; now, no cloth of gold
  By modern Launcelot is won; the art
Of courtesy refined, that Queen Anne bore,
 That Fielding penned, and Ivanhoe once told,
  Is past and gone—a jewel without a mart!

THE DECAY OF CHIVALRY.

AND why is chivalry no more?   It is because
  Man has given up the effeminate ideal,
  His Magdalen of purity.   Men feel
Not with the old love patriarchal laws
  Laid down !   The chain of family tie—
  Through courtesy not going with chastity—
Has snapped.   Parental homage no more draws
The conscience young ; self triumphs, not the cause
Of virtue chivalrous—offspring of home !
  Shattered is man's ideal in womankind
    Through age of "Rights,"that tossed now on the wave
Of doubt, his idol gives he up !   No longer roam
  His thoughts to heaven, cynic he's grown in mind,
    A creature " of the world" on to the grave.

THE REVIVAL OF CHIVALRY.

MAN's tabernacle must be purified,
　　And mental culture grow with moral code,
　　If progress is to lead us on the road
To deeds of chivalry anew !　The pride
Of hopeless cynics must be laid aside
　　Ere Nature's gentlehood spring from the wreck
　　Of courtly laws !　More light must come to deck
The new Madonna ere she's heaven's bride !
A firmer, nobler faith, that will not fail,
　　Must be disclosed.　Science with her strong arm
　　Must yet unfold more of the hidden light
Masking life's mystery "behind the veil : "
　　Then deeds of chivalry will come to charm
　　　The gentle fair ones from the gallant knight !

CHEERFULNESS.

He has a mine of wealth whose cup runs o'er
   With cheerfulness; whose genial manners grace
   His being with a smile, light up his face
With calm contentment; out of Nature's store
No lasting attribute of man can pour
   A richer meed of pleasure; from its well
   No waters sparkle like its bright jets, tell
Such conquests of the heart, so heavenwards soar !

He wastes a day who never deigns to laugh,
   Loses a friend that greets not with a smile,
And forfeits bliss who still declines to quaff
   Its living and reviving nectar !   'Tis the stile
That leads our footfalls o'er the bridge of sighs
Into health's home, sustains us as life flies !

A ROSE.

EMBLEM of love, grafted on fancy's wings
  In grove of Eden long ago, the flower
  By maids enamoured, pride of the Giaour,
Queen of the garden! In thy beauty kings
Have paid thee homage ; of all offerings
  At shrine of love thy sweetness stands apart,
  As attar does its scent ! No Cupid's dart
Can slay as thou ! No fonder whisper brings
Thy cup of tint to maiden ; in the form
  Of eglantine, thy petals pure array
  The retinue of brides ! Sweet is thy spray—
Whether of gold or blush ! thou dost conform
  To deck all ceremonial ; no bloom,
  Like thine, shows love or friendship at the tomb !

THE GREAT PYRAMID.

THERE it stands, the weird colossal pile!
   A monument of labour mocking time,
   A Cyclops in the desert, sultry clime
Of Pharaoh's land, close to the silvery Nile—
Ages unborn, new races to beguile!
   Terrace on terrace quite two hundred odd,
   Capped by a crystal, go to make the god,
And seal o'er the king's chamber and its aisle!

Weapons of beryl, sapphire, hewed the block
   And picked the mammoth stones that make the mass!
Tablets of marble, stones from Sinai's rock,
   Adorn the shrine where destined had to pass
The sacred relics of Egyptian kings,
Safe from the caliphs and the vulture's wings!

THE GREAT PYRAMID: A MOCKER
OF TIME!

The Roman Colosseum's ruined walls,
   The Athenian temple of Minerva wise,
   Point to the glory gone of centuries
In history's page ; their stately columns, halls,
Both testify to ruin that befalls
   The piles of time ; yet Cheops' great design,
   Like to the work of Architect divine,
Enjoys perennial youth, and mind enthralls
With wondrous awe ; for forty centuries long
   The massive mound sepulchral has held sway
Over the Libyan sands, and Bedouin song
   Its hallowed past proclaims unto this day :
It stands a masterpiece of every age,
Its founder's genius baffles sage on sage !

THE SPHINX.

FRONTING the Pyramids the great Sphinx lies,
  A rock-hewn monster of immortal fame,
  Buried beneath the sand to fane proclaim,
On ground once sacred to the Ptolemies !
To guard the treasure-house of mysteries ;
  Barbaric effigy she stands, to thrill
  Mankind as giant from the Libyan hill,
And age and pagan ruin both defies !

Orbless, austere, but ever vigilant,
  The queen of terrors guards the massive piles,
Mock-sentinel 'gainst fate, and seems to chant
  Her founder's prayer against Egyptian wiles :
"Worship, ye caliphs ! for I watch on them—
Your kings—now dead, who wore your diadem ! "

MAY-DAY.

IT is the first of May, when Nature pants
　　With joy and gladness, and the emerald bloom
　　Of nestled foliage leaves the Winter's tomb
Of rest; when vegetation's sportive prance
Through native force begins; when waking earth
　　Puts on her tresses of luxuriant hue,
　　To pay the debt of gentle Spring—now due,
Ere yielding forth the Summer's floral birth!

We hail thee, May bloom! May tree! lily May!
　　We greet thy blossoms, buds, thy peeping leaves;
Thy bursts of growth unfolding cheer our day
　　With hope of risen life—our bosom heaves;
　　We are reminded of the Summer sheaves
Of plenty, and so, bless thee, glorious May!

SPRING.

NATURE is now awake, and genial Spring
  With fragrant bursting foliage greets the morn
  With virgin freshness ; countless birds new-born
Are in full song ; the bee and everything
Possessing sense and life's awakening ;
  Blackthorn and cherry, lilac, groves adorn,
  Snowdrops and daffodils the woods forlorn ;
Thrushes and starlings now are on the wing.

The chiff-chaff monotones, the willow-wren
  Steals back unnoticed from its Afric nest
To twitter with the robin in the glen ;
  The wagtail courts the plough, the lark—earth's best
Of vocalists—to heaven its song uprears,
And Spring to everything man's soul endears !

THE FORCE OF NATURE.

O FORCE inscrutable! whence dost thou come?
  From heaven, or from that glowing influence, light
  Of Sol's ecliptic path? Circle of might,
Phenomenon celestial! We are dumb,
And cannot trace thy essence, soul of Spring!
  That clothes the mead with grass, the landscape fills
With beauty, fragrance gives and colouring
  To petals, rears the kine, the mind instils
With wisdom, drives the sap, makes lion roar
  With lusty furor, antelopes with grace
Nigh acrobatic, fishes swim, birds soar
  Towards empyrean. Intellects all face
And analyse in vain thy subtle power,
Veiled source of life, creation, heavenly dower!

SUMMER: GROWTH.

A CEASELESS wave of motion guides the growth
  Of foliage and flower; sweet streams of sap
  Build cell on cell of bud; from Winter's nap
Chrome granules spring from cells and nourish both
The blade and bloom; the sun, no longer loth
  To pour his genial rays, expands the ears
  Of golden corn till harvest-tide appears;
Matter and motion kiss, and plight their troth!

Fruits, flowers, and leaves all revel in the feast
  Of Nature's dance; life springs up in the mead,
Birds in the air, and mites—greatest and least
  Of things created on its bounties feed:
Growth glads the rushes, roses, robins, flowers;
'Tis matter swayed by motion through Sol's powers!

SUMMER: THE HUMBLE-BEE.

THINK of the homeless, happy humble-bee,
  Sipping the floral nectar from the flowers!
  No hive has he to shield him in the showers;
He is a type of flower-time.   Watch his glee,
  As his broad tawny frame glides buoyantly
Across the mead to buttercup, then elm,
Then off to lilac, then to other realm,
  Flower-fertilising mite of industry!

Restless and wild, but so endowed with sense,
  He visits, like a charmer, glen and heath,
Gathering their floral sweets with diligence
  Into his basket—quite a fairy sheath!
His ceaseless brush plies on from morn till night;
He never wastes a moment in time's flight!

SUMMER: ITS FLOOD OF LIFE.

No feast of life a season e'er reveals
  Like Summer !   Let us wander to a mead
  And note its plenty, see the insects feed
With ceaseless din on dainties, watch the meals
Of scaly flies, grasshoppers, as each feels
  The sweetness of the virgin blade, the flower
  Ere by the sickle felled ; earth's vital power
With movement is astir, o'er all things steals !

The May-flower's fallen, but the oak's new leaves
  Are bursting forth, clover and daisy blooms
Now hide the skylark, as with skill he weaves
  His nest ; bees spring from larval tombs ;
O'erhead the swallow darts with noisy scream,
And life's aglow with glee in solar beam !

SUMMER: INSECTS AND BIRDS.

CREATURES of purpose dark bask in the glow
 And flood of solar beam ; beside the copse
 Flutters the butterfly, around tree-tops
Dense clouds of young gnats buzz, and just below
Brown chafers feed, and beetles in a row
 Across the footpath speed ; the dragon-fly
 With iridescent scales darts furiously
Off to yon lake, where swallows hover low !

The stillness of the air is broken by the crake
 Of landrail in the long-grown grass ; the wren
Sings from the weeping willow by the lake !
 Grasshoppers chirp all day in yonder glen ;
Swarms of strange life of Nature's fruits partake,
 And odious creatures thrive that baffle ken !

SUMMER: THE BIRDS.

THE song of birds now fills the azure air !
 List to the green finch piping to his love
 In yonder hawthorn bough, and high above
To the sleek blackbird's trill, as from his lair
He echo waits from loving mate up there !
 The yellow-hammer sings till autumn's sheaf
 Is garnered, till the rustle's heard of leaf,
And notes from linnets, tits, sound everywhere !

Like to the cadence of a waterfall,
 The songs of thrushes rise and sink at morn,
Pausing like chiff-chaffs when to loves they call !
 Whitethroats and cuckoos now the air adorn :
For mimicry and love, swifts, skylarks, pour
Forth rival song on woodland, stream, and moor !

SUMMER: A GALA-TIME.

THE pulse of youth now throbs to hie from school
　　Into the country fields, to wickets drive
　　Into the sward; young men and maidens strive
With bat and ball at net, and play's the rule
Of life! Some row along the stream for cool
　　And gentle pastime; on the river's bank
　　Pleasure's the aim of life of every rank,
And youths of spirit dive into the pool!

Health, mirth, and hope spring from the long warm day,
　　Both young and old drink in the gentle breeze!
Man's spirits, like the lark's, fly heavenwards gay,
　　Thanks to the beams of light, the wave of trees!
All life seems bent on mingling in the dance
Of Summer's pageant and of youth's romance!

SUMMER: A COSY RIVER'S NOOK.

Posies of wild-flowers scent the river's brink,
   Poppies and marguerite from sword-flags peep,
   And loosestrife red springs from the watery deep;
Behind the willow's thicket lychnis pink
May be espied, where moorhens come to drink!
   The hart's-tongue fern nestles beneath the bank,
   Safe from the wind and sun, 'neath bulrush lank—
There waterlilies' cups now rise and sink!

The ruby trefoil tints the adjoining mead,
   And banquets hives of bees and butterflies;
Beneath the tangled hedge the bluebell's seed
   Sprinkles the moss; above wild roses rise,
And blooms of honeysuckle twine round may,
Wafting the fragrance of a rich nosegay!

NATURE IN JULY.

Month of the rose, the butterfly, the oak,
  Season of warblers, whitethroats, birds whose chant
  Makes tangled hedges, trout-streams, eloquent
With song, proclaim thyself!   No glory cloak
Of floral bloom, insect, or bird ; convoke
The powers of Nature, operatic gift
  Of finches green, of skylarks, pipits, give
To rambler man ; with dart and chirp of swift,
  Martins, and swallows, make the air alive
With voice ; to canopy of heaven uplift
  Pæan of linnet, hum of humble-bee,
Loud cry of timid landrail, quaintest voice
  Of whinchat, churr of nightjar, whizzing glee
Of insects basking heavenwards—Earth rejoice !

ASTRONOMICAL.

AIR-GIRDLED orb of life and love, the sphere
  Of ceaseless charm, of products bountiful,
  Poised in the planes of space, of order full,
Whirl cycling on in path majestic, veer
Round to Sol's glorious rays, each day endear
  At summer solstice life to us, then on
  Obliquely roll past thine aphelion !
That man, bird, beast, and fish, peasant and peer,
May flourish in *rotation*, all rejoice
  In latitudes benign.　Aerial dew
Fall gently in thy cataract, thy tears
  On British landscape !　Erebus, thy voice
Of thunder dire restrain, thy bolts subdue
Towards vegetation, now July appears.

A DREAM OF AUTUMN.

THE harvest moon had risen ; I was asleep,
  Wrapped in delicious reverie, whirled away
  To hall baronial where a roundelay
From merry maidens echoed—feast to keep
Of harvest-tide : plenty, that all might reap,
  Had filled the earth ; rustic and courtly squire
  Had come to chant their joy ; cymbal and lyre,
Guitar, lute, zither, swelled an anthem deep !

The patron saint was there ; incense arose
  From urns suspended from the lofty dome ;
  Garlands of flowers festooned the hall, the home
Of thanksgiving—poppy, clematis, rose,
  And fruit and corn !—when I awoke, to find
  That bronze leaves fluttered in the morning wind !

AUTUMN : DECAY OF THE FLOWERS.

THE children of the sun now droop, the lily's cup
  Inverts its petals, blue lobelia's tost
  And wildly torn, geranium's beauty's lost.
Few are the flowers the bee now deigns to sup,
The sunflower flags, clematis' glories wane,
  The purple foxglove, harebell, yellow broom
On bracken flourish, heath, elecampane
  Grow wild on moor, no longer roses bloom,
Queen Flora lays her sceptre down, and seeks
  A southern home ! Crimson and brown and gold
  Have petals left for leaves ; few flowers are bold
Or strong enough to sport their tinted cheeks !
  A cold wind murmurs through dismantled trees,
  And soon King Frost will come all things to freeze !

AUTUMN : OTHER CHANGES.

NATURE her russet robes has now put on,
 Bewitching colour tints the fading leaves,
 The reaper's task is done, and Ceres' sheaves
Are husbanded—Summer has clearly gone !
Welcome, October, nut-brown earth upon !
 Change though there be in wood and lane and field,
 Wealth and a mine of form the seasons yield,
Whether in town, where'er the sun has shone !

The force of Nature's spent, the genial sun
 Has wandered 'neath the line—a biting air
 Crumples the withering foliage, trees lays bare ;
In chestnut, oak, and elm the sap's begun
 To seek the ground, the equinoctial gale
 Havoc in forest plays, on hill and dale !

AUTUMN : THE LAST LEAF.

DISROBED and unadorned, the trees assume
  A witchery of grace ; the golden grey
  Tresses that herald, beautify decay,
Nature puts off, and gathers to the tomb
Of rest ; a purpose wise foretells the doom
  Of verdure ; wealth of flower and leaf
  Is first showered forth, then garnered with the sheaf
Of harvest—beauty both of blade and bloom !

Decay thus follows growth, that earth in sleep
  May capillary sap attract from trees
  To force conserve till peep of Spring from breeze
Of Winter dire, that life may vigour keep.
  The last leaf falls ! the twigs stand out with grace !
  'Tis Nature resting for a little space !

AUTUMN : MIGRATION OF THE BIRDS.

BIRDS from the moor, the forest, seck retreat,
   The linnets, twites, and wagtails leave the gorse
   For sheltered glens, the plovers have recourse
To cosier homes !   Buntings and chaffinch fleet,
Sparrows and finches green, the stubble beat
   Ere flitting ; rooks now revel in the elms,
   While wrens and chiff-chaffs go to warmer realms ;
Nor is the flock of migrants yet complete !

Fraternity, while hovering in the air,
   Seek the wild heron and the curlew shrill ;
Both gulls and larks with dunlins, warblers, pair,
   While harsh screams come from migrants o'er the hill :
Falcons and owls no longer stop to prey
On smaller tribe while crossing Biscay's Bay !

AUTUMN : THE HUSH OF SONG.

HUSHED are the songs that cheered our hearts in Spring,
  With jubilee at dawn, with serenade—
  Those matin-songs that filled both home and glade
Welled forth by warblers newly on the wing !
Has bird-life sung its dirge, that vocal ring
  Is still ? Or has its song with young ones fled
  At fall ? The berry's mellow, ripe, and red,
And fruit and corn in plenty seasons bring ;
Yet a sad stillness reigns, the yellow leaf
  Crumples and falls—rustling a requiem ;
  The trees stand forth as fretwork in the stem,
And birds' plumes fall with man's locks to the sheaf
  Of Time's keen scythe.   Yes, climes in cycles run,
  And all life wanes with Autumn's setting sun !

AUTUMN: THE BIRDS.

COUNCIL is held aloft in air 'mong tribe
  Of Summer migrants now autumnal chill
  Sets in ; martins' and swallows' voices shrill
Are heard aloft, fledglings and mates to bribe
To warmer climes ; the goldcrests now subscribe
  Their twitters to the coppice, wee blue tits
  Echo in thickets to the robin's twits ;
The wren at home, whose song pen can't describe,
Or beauty, stays !   From bracken skylarks rise,
  And mussel-thrushes, pipits leave the gorse !
  Sparrows and finches green the stubble course
To carol forth autumnal melodies !
  Into the covey runs the partridge shy,
  T' escape the spaniel or the sportsman's eye !

AUTUMN: A GALE.

CRASH went the chimney-top, off flew the tiles
  On to the flags below, loud howled the trees,
  Pelted the rain ; a stiff autumnal breeze
Grew to a gale ; the thunderstorm the piles
  Made totter ! Just as though the air to clear
Of pestilence—'twere needed, trees of leaves
  Should be stripped, whirled away this time of year
In one fell swoop ! No wonder man's breast heaves
  With anxious fears ; still Nature's laws will go
Uncheck'd ; the flowers, the fruits, must flourish, run
  Their course ! The tides were settled long ago !
    Decay must follow growth in life and sense ;
Sojourn elsewhere's a portion of the sun,
  Whose bounty signifies omnipotence.

A SUNSET OFF THE WASH.

'TWAS off the Wash I saw the sun go down,
  A glorious ball of fire, dazzling to sight
  And decked with coruscating rays of light,
That cast a mirror on the sea; to crown
The spectacle, the sky had ne'er a frown,
  No angry cumulus its pale blue vault
  Obscured; the sea was calm, without a fault,
A crimson lake the heavens ranged to brown!

Then inch by inch his photosphere through haze
  Diminished in its glory, in its play
    Of colour on the horizon, like a dome
Of some grand Eastern kiosk set ablaze;
  He now sank low, and waned the light of day.
    I cried out, "Ichabod!" and wandered home.

WINTER : MIGRATION OF THE BIRDS.

YET some birds still sing on in spite of rain
   And biting cold of winter; the pet bird,
   The robin, e'en in hoar-frost's often heard
Trilling in copse his sweet yet plaintive strain !
The restless jenny-wren, who will oft remain,
   From icicle-clad branch makes glad the air,
   Succeeded by the starling from his lair,
Although the nightingale's on Afric's plain !

Song-thrushes, buntings, snowy vales ne'er heed,
   Redwings and pipits still the thicket shields,
While swifts and swallows to the South now speed.
   Mysterious instinct this, to seek these fields !
Music and mirth skylarks and finches pour,
Heedless of frost and snow, o'er hill and moor !

WINTER : BEAUTY AND USE OF.

THE wealth of foliage Nature gave she takes
    Back to her bosom, Autumn's glory wanes,
    And icy beads now deck the window-panes ;
Snow stainless strews the ground, and fleecy flakes
Like swansdown fall; the waggon-wheel large cakes
    Picks up and scatters !   Tinkle of falling snow
    From the weird trees responds to bitter blow ;
The east wind cuts the land, the homestead shakes.

Meridian's splendour's dim—the days are short,
    Yet Winter has its joys in spite of dearth—
Age at the hearth, and youth without in sport,
    Harvest's been garnered in for Christmas mirth :
Frost binds, yet lightens, vigour 'tis to soil,
Sleep and nutrition till the next year's toil !

WINTER : HOME-BIRDS.

THE fall of leaf and harvest's now complete,
   And warblers few in shrubberies remain ;
   The flocks are in Algeria, some in Spain.
But jays and blackbirds scorn to make retreat,
Finches and tits, woodpeckers still we meet,
   Dipper, and him of chestnut, blue, and green—
   Kingfisher of the brook's the bird I mean !
And wagtails haunt our homes, the snow and sleet :
Along the coast snow-bunting's to be found,
   And graceful snipes cosy 'neath grassy tents ;
Sandpipers, curlews, on our shores abound,
   And mavis sings at times with eloquence :
On to our doorstep oft the robin comes,
To vie with sparrows for the scattered crumbs.

TO THE STATUE OF "THE LADY" IN MILTON'S "COMUS."

THERE she sits—a queen of all the graces, bound
    To marble chair through sorcerer—Comus' wand !
    Forsaken by her brothers, left to band
Of fiendish revellers, whose rustic sound
Has lured her in the wood !   Looking around
    Disconsolate, she cries, "Sabrina, save !"   Her song
    Brings Comus ; then her brothers come along,
And dash th' envenomed philtre to the ground
The fiend had lured her with !   Thyrsis' device
    Unheeded went, to seize the juggler's wand
        That chained her to the rock ; Sabrina, born
Of Locrine famed, could solely in a trice
    Uncharm the wand.   She came ; her hand
        Sprinkled, caressed, and freed the queen forlorn !

THE BLIND GIRL, "NYDIA."

" Hush ! stand aside, the sweet Thessalian maid,
  The blind girl Nydia, trips along, my slave,
  Scattering her posies on the floor with wave
Of service glad !" the Athenian Glaucus said :
And with her basket full of flowers, arrayed
  In lily-white, the shy and faltering
  Nymph with a mien upborne, her steps feeling,
Entered the hall with song, and homage paid !

Drop tears of grief, unfreeze your hearts of stone,
  Ye readers of romance, on this poor girl !
    Slave to a magnate of Pompeii, born
To grace a throne, life beautify, not one
    To lavish on a Greek !   Her deeds unfurl
    A soul's in gloom, past history adorn !

PHILOSOPHY OF BIRDS' SONG.

WHAT is the meaning of thy lyrics, trills
   Of melody, thy echoes, bird of song?
   Is it the eloquence of language strong
In fervour to thy mate that welling fills
Thy bosom with delight? or is't that thrills
   Of ecstasy instinctive in thee rise
   To glorify man's life, to fill the skies
With notes so sweet that other Jacks and Jills
   May thy love's plaint find echo, and inspire,
   In aviary of Nature, other choir
To feats of love?   Methinks thy gleeful tone,
   Thy carol on thy perch of pride, thy joy,
   Is fittest of thy feathered mate t' enjoy
In courtship, songster! 'Tis romance alone!

MOTIVE OF BIRDS' SONG.

YE meadow-larks, ye blue-birds, and ye jays,
  Ye mocking-birds, ye nightingales so sweet,
  With chaffinch, jenny-wren, with pretty tweet!
Why matin songs at dewy morn, why lays
Do ye pour forth? Is't emulation's ways
  That fittest may survive? or that thy breast
  Is piping far too full to take a rest
In seeking mate and ties 'fore Autumn days,
  That progeny may linger in the vale
  With voice to swell the joy of sylvan dale
Anon? What is't, sweet birds, so merrily
  That ye sing on, so saucily, so hale,
In timbre lyrical, unless it be
  That habit is thy instinct—Mimicry!

THE SUN : ITS POWER.

O GREAT and mighty globe ! vast source of life
  And fiery incandescence, scene of roar
  Of rushing heat and cyclone ! we adore
Thy splendour, power, magnificence ; thy strife
Of molten elements, thy rage is rife
  With purpose ! for all finished planets whirl
  Around thee circling, all of which unfurl
Due glory at due distance.   Some with life
Are credited.   Mars, Jove, all planets rise
  And set, obedient to thy decrees—
  Repulsion, gravitation !   Galaxies
Of starry realms attest thy might, thy loss
  Of vast effulgence ; facts—all mysteries
Till solved by thy rotation, Helios !

THE SUN : ITS COMBUSTION.

THY hell-like blasts, thy hurricanes of fire,
   Thy giant throes of glowing lava, storms
Of matter, conflagration, all conspire
   To turn thee on thine axis!   Mighty forms
Of energy pervade thy mass, thy might,
   That, seething, seek supremacy!   Forces
Imprisoned elements among, all fight
With ceaseless roar; in that orbs' destinies
   Without may be controlled in mighty swoop,
And other stellar worlds their distance keep,
Infinity of space and asteroids reap
   Illumination, force, capacity
To keep attraction's laws, and life recoup
   Its energy through thy fecundity!

THE SUN : ITS FATE.

THY heat, light, bounty, glorious Sol ! thy power,
   Contraction, revolution, life-gift, birth
   To family of suns, to asteroids, earth !
We recognise as government supreme, as dower
Celestial ! Streams of radiation, shower
   On shower of matter meteoric show
   Thy boundless wealth of energy ! Thy bow
Of tint prismatic, that 'mid rain doth tower
Above, attests thy glory up on high !
   All things must die ! Thy photosphere of light,
Corona, spots volcanic, testify,
   Sun-god ! through lens of spectrum, that thy might
Will wane, mass fade away, and that thy face
Will one day fail t' illume e'en human race !

THE SUN: SEQUEL TO EXTINCTION.

FIRE-LADEN ruler of the earth! vast sun,
  Giver of all things, source of golden beams,
  Of motion, matter, and of sense! death seems
A judgment far too terrible, for none
Of starry empires, satellites, would run
  Their course, 'twould seem again, survive thy fate,
  The extinction of thy force! Mind can't create
Order without thee; life would be undone!

Thou art the "All" within the solar planes;
  No matter what thine end, whether thy vast
Empire do smoulder, freeze, no orb remains
  Like thine beneath heaven's dome! Such end,
      such blast,
Must bring annihilation to the face
Of Nature, wreck all worlds, cosmos displace!

ON A BUTTERFLY.

'Tis but a butterfly! that loves the sun,
  And gambols in the glow of summer-time
  In quest of native nectar—food sublime
For gods and insects; all winged things that run
Their course ephemeral, like Cupid, shun
  Aught but the sweets of life, the floral lips
  Of peeping blossoms!   Flitting fly, that skips
From flower to flower, whose life, ere yet begun,
Is doomed to end—'tis a White Admiral!
  Perched on a twig of honeysuckle, leaf
To palpi savoury, and bloom withal
  Pungent as lilies in a floral sheaf—
That courts my Muse, that zigzag seeks the sky,
Type of a risen life—though but a butterfly!

THE BUTTERFLY: ITS DEVELOPMENT.

TRANSITION full of mystery! First egg,
   Then creeping state, then chrysalis, then change
   To perfect insect—parts replete with range
Of faculty, of sense, to explore the keg
   Of floral nectar—the gay butterfly,
   With scaly wings, like jewels to the eye,
Appears at last in beauty, freed from skin,—
   Relic of larva, transformation strange!
Type of a life evolved from force within
   Cocoon! Each state, each subtle interchange
Foretells man's destiny! The creeping stage—
   His life on earth; the chrysalis—his tomb
Of rest this side the veil, his hermitage;
   The perfect insect—life beyond the gloom!

ON A FLY.

(IN FLY LORE.)

I AM a little fly !—a buzzing, rambling pest
 Some call me !   Simple, two-winged happy mite
 Perched on two balancers, with gift of sight
My giddy head can scarcely hold—two peepers blest
With mighty range of vision in the quest
 Of hidden dainties, hue of chocolate :
 I love excursions—to a fly innate—
And oft go chevy-chase, sweets to digest
Or mate to torment with my two-lobed tongue,
 "Ah, there's the rub !" which like a file can pick
 To pieces anything that's savoury—a trick
I can perform, when topsy-turvy hung
 From ceiling by my hairy padded feet !
 My joy's a summer's span : then life's complete !

．

ON A DRAGON-FLY.

A VISION.

SEE from yon floating plant creep out, from husk
  Already sun-dried, the awed dragon-fly !
  Scorning its wintry suit of clothes, the dry
And hardened hermit of a life that dusk
  Alone enjoyed ! Fierce mite, green-eyed, with wings
Light as the finest gauze, with aureole flecked ;
  Nigh iridescent, trunk of sapphire rings
Glittering all over like a jewel, decked
A very king of insects ! See him dart
  From flag of bulrush, cross yon stream, and shoot
    His animated mask at butterfly
Making for distant mead ! Poor heart,
  That thy gay wings, thy limbs, should thus by root
    Be plucked, devoured by tyrant dragon-fly !

THE PRICE OF A PEEP.

(ACROSTICAL.)

(Written in a Young Lady's Album.)

CONDITIONS fixed await all those who look
   On these fair pages—mint of all that's chaste !
   None of its jewels set in fancy's taste,
None of the mental gems that deck my book
I'll have ta'en out "to hang on other's hook,"
   E'en at the price of dearest friendship, love !
   So say I ! Feast herein, but don't remove
Heart-throbbings set to verse from any nook !

Entreaty two : I court in blank and rhyme,
   Prose, epic, lyric—aught in poetry ;
   Promptings by fancy, art, wit, memory,
Also original in mode and time.
   Remember this ! For peeping here, the price
   Declared of all's, to write me something nice !

TO THE SUNDEW.

(DROSERA ROTUNDIFOLIA.)

THOU honey-laden hair and dew clad flower,
   Sister of Dionæa ! what strange freak
   Of Nature raised thy being from the meek?
What means thy vegetal digestive power?
Does sense along thy fibrils dawn—the dower
   Of feeling? or do thread-like nerves find trace
   Within thy leaves of pile, that court th' embrace
Of merry mites of flight?   O fatal bower !
Thy craft belies thy innocence, thy bait
   Of nectared juice is but a crafty trap
To lure winged life and bring about its fate !
   Two worlds of being thou bridgest o'er—the gap
'Tween animal and plant !   A peptic bond
Links thee with jelly-fish and life beyond !

A SPIDER'S WEB: MECHANISM.

ANCHORED 'mid leafy twigs, her home is set
  In gossamer—spun from a dorsal crest
  Of microscopic tubes—the spider's best
Arts have instinctively framed to a net
Of silk.   Some call her gland a spinnaret!
  The building thus begins; the central part
  Of mooring seeks she out, alone to start
To part opposed—diameter to get.

Backward she runs half-way and spins her threads
  Distinct from line she's on to circle reach,
    And radii make complete by pulling taut;
Retracing steps ere spinning, then she treads
  Her way to centre radial to each,
    Pulling each faultless spoke till all are wrought!

A SPIDER'S WEB: MECHANISM—(continued).

SAMPLER of Nature beautiful!   A wheel
   With radii twenty-six is first laid down
   Before the lines concentric come to crown
Arachne's work, who spins away with zeal
From her resources—for her future weal—
   Her non-adhesive matter, dry and tough ;
   The web's now fairly finished in the rough.
The architect next spins right off the reel
Adhesive substance spiral lines along,
   In globules glistening—prey to enfold
   In mesh elastic ; circles manifold
Go to complete the task, the web make strong :
   For seven-and-eighty thousand cells are spun
   In minutes forty-five, ere task is done !

THE LUSTRE OF SIRIUS.

SKIRTING Orion's belt, great Sirius reigns
   The brightest star in heaven, of suns a king,
And giant amid orbs! but poised in planes
   None but astronomers can gauge, ruling
A galaxy of glory, wielding sway
   O'er systems vaster than the solar grand!
Light-shedding, heat-eclipsing orb of day,
   Would that thy full powers we could understand!

But since design governs terrestrial law,
   Thy planes, O Sirius! surely must enjoy
     Floræ and faunæ, force exceeding far
Vast Sol's domain!   Proud sophist, man, withdraw
   Thy concepts crude of space!   Thy world's a toy
     Compared e'en with these orbs ruled by this star!

LIFE IN OTHER WORLDS.

THINK not, proud earthly man, finite in mind,
   This world we tread on's but the sole abode
   Of life.   Races of men exist on orbs that load
The empyrean! Brilliants a Ross can find
That dissipate old notions of mankind
   Concerning life! Think of Aldebaran,
   Prince Betelgeux ruling Orion's span
In ether veiled! Where air is, life's combined.

Venus, air-laden, mankind's home must prove,
   And heat, obliquely shed, give life on Mars;
Set forms of vital force must reign on Jove,
   Or why such pomp and retinue 'mid stars?
Vast types of life, as here, exist afar
In sea of space, suited to plane and star!

LIFE IN OTHER WORLDS: MORAL !

Sink, man, your jealousy !   Dry well your eyes,
  Thou, hitherto but heaven's earthly love,
  Hast thus so late such rivals !   God above
Er said " He'd many mansions in the skies "
Through the Apostle John !   Eternities
  Of life and home were meant, where greater bliss
  May possibly be man's in quitting this—
Think of the risen life of butterflies !

The lilies toil not, neither do they spin,
  Yet in their seed's a glorious heritage !
Potential force may bear, as acorns in,
  Creations lovelier than on mankind's page ;
First Cause all-powerful can alone evolve
Stages of life anew, soul's mystery solve !

A ROYAL WEDDING.

July 27, 1889.

HAIL, Royal Princess and favoured Duke of Fife,
  To court of Hymen called!   Flutter on towers,
  Ye flags; ye clarions sound, invoke the powers
Of benediction all on husband, wife,
Linked with approval popular and rife
  With seal of truest love!   Britain, rejoice!
  One of your kin has gained the Sovereign's choice:
Ring out your salvoes for their happy life!

Sink, highly cultured nymph, your Royal claim
  To court distinction now!   Be your desire,
    In close alliance with a noble clan,
To footsteps follow of great mother's fame,
  "Sweetness and light" to find.   Great Duke, aspire
    A nation's trust to merit!   Happy man!

ON SLEEP.

O CALM of each day's toil, new life-gift, Sleep!
  Goddess of sable night, that doth transport
  Us weary pilgrims to oblivion's port!
Who doth not feel thy grateful powers at peep
Of day?   Who to thy realm from care won't creep
  At faintest bidding, find a lullaby?
  Youth gleans a power to conquer ills well-nigh
O'erwhelming under thee in learning's steep!

Thou art the architect of rugged health,
  Agility of limb, good spirits, mind
    In its activity.   None need disdain
Thy long embrace, for truth to thee means wealth:
  Then let us use thee well, long life to find
    Ere we sleep on, never to wake again!

PART III.

Miscellaneous Poems.

LEAFY JUNE.

Fair month of bloom, of beauty, and of beam,
'Tis in thy lap we feast most amply, seem
To feel the spell of Paradise below.
The azure sky above proclaims thy bow,
Thy flood of bounty, fleecy clouds despite,
And fleeting cumuli.   Such is thy might
To shed abroad Sol's streams of glowing rays.
How the earth revels in thy gladsome days!
Buds now unfolding glad the sloping meads,
And everywhere we see Spring's doughty deeds
Bearing rich flower and fruit.   The grass has grown,
Daisies and buttercups their blooms have shown,

And trees are being robed for Nature's dance,
As sprites of beauty from a Winter's trance !
Thou leafy month of joy ! who wouldn't watch
Thy tints of splendour grow?   Who fain could match
Or emulate thy grace?   No queen of State
Or rustic beauty of a fancy fête
Can deck with taste like thine, so well put on
Her tresses, suited to Hyperion !
No perfume heavenward floats like to thy flowers,
Whether from primrose bank or lilac bowers,
Wafted by zephyrs or by fleeting showers.

There's music in the rustling of thy leaves,
Attuned in length to song until the sheaves
Are ready for the sickle.   How the bees
On meads of clover revel, sing their glees !
Atoms of Summer whisper all the day,
And testify to Flora's pageant gay.
Hope fills Dame Nature's heart, and all the earth
Is in full travail to be giving birth
To her dear children, to restore anew
To man and beasts the fruits that now are due !

List to the nightingale !   He's now "at home ;"
Though sadly driven oft by man to roam,
He's in the coppice yon.   How tender, sad,
His liquid note resounds, then turns to glad
Notes of sweet treble !   I have often stood
And listened to this songster of the wood,
Dumb-struck, attentive to his vocal scale,
Instinct with language : "That's a lover's tale,"

Has been my whisper ! Then I've trudged along,
And mused upon the riches of his song,
Brighter for hearing it. Have birds a soul,
That thus their warblings through our senses roll ?
You list for answer. You will list in vain ;
But surely Paradise they'd not profane.
May's now attired in pink, and cherry's white
Blossoms of bridal buds are quite a sight ;
The opening fans of elms and chestnuts grace
The verdant mead, the glen, man's dwelling-place.

Look where we may, the bursting leaf arrests
Our orbs of wonder. Oh, the countless nests
Thy blades will help to hide ! What chattering glee
Will issue soon from yonder well-branched tree !
An emerald garb the hedges now assume
To hide the birds in rivalry of plume,
And trysting-place of love ! The dog-rose there
In wild luxuriance opes its buds with care ;
The fervour of the impassioned regal sun
Unfolds its bridal petals every one ;
Nothing so loved as budding eglantine
Along the tangled thicket is e'er seen,
Save honeysuckle's tendrils crisp and sweet,
Whose clinging blooms our senses always greet.
Not to forget the little woodruff's face,
And blue forget-me-nots of sweetest grace ;
They grow for happy lovers, gems of bloom,
Omens of constancy, till crack of doom !

No wonder Wordsworth spoke so touchingly
Anent " the meanest flower " that grows hard by

The sheltered bracken !   But his favourite child
Was Nature, chaste, luxuriant, wild.
The emerald vestments charm the feathered tribe
Whose songs to solar glory we ascribe.
The wary throstle on the verdant mead
Now struts in safety, fledglings soon to feed ;
A merry chorus shakes the matin-breeze,
Such is the joy of warblers in the trees !
The very wind is charged with living force
To fructify earth's flowers along its course ;
Dust rich in pollen floats in waves along,
Attuned to hum of bees and feathered song ;
The very atmosphere's a living thing,
For in its atoms seeds are on the wing.
Life leaps in joy from gambolling mites below
To diving migrants feasting in the glow
Of solar beams.   Each floret and each leaf
Appears to sing, " I live again, in brief."
From oak to bird, from bird to butterfly,
The selfsame song is chanted in the sky,
And man the spell of the Immortals feels
When all this transport o'er his senses steals !

The little whitethroat twitters near the pond,
And bids his sitting mate to ne'er despond ;
He scolds, he carols, flits as with a jerk,
And seems to sing, " My duty I'll not shirk ; "
Then to the apple-tree flies the next minute
To seek the company of lonely linnet.
From flowering green sward now you'll often see
The chaffinch on a hedge perched saucily,

Fluting a solo to a lady-love,
Whose nestling duties prompt her not to move.
Nature's *en fête*, for is there not a sound,
A hum of music in the breezes found?
The very grasses sing, the hedges creak,
The pulse of Nature beats and seems to speak
In terms of thankfulness to Sol's full beams
For waking slumbering life from Winter dreams.

The very sorrel-spires drink in the wine
Distilled by sunshine, golden buttercups
The while participating; daisies bold
Now vie quite perkily with flowers of gold;
The vault of heaven inspires the lark to song,
Whose lovely warble oft seems tried too long.
Go where you will, the landscape gives you joy,
And often helps life's burdens to alloy.
Off to the clover-fields now swarms of bees
Hasten, when tired of sipping apple-trees;
Clear of the thicket you may see them fly,
As though to lose no time across the sky.
But Nature's sterner forces oft prevail
To mar June's splendour—thunderstorm and hail
To wreck its fête-like pageant, cloud its face,
Though gala's soon restored to human race:
The storm's no sooner o'er, the clouds at rest,
Than out the starling flits with speckled breast;
The solar beams no sooner glad the air
Than all the birds come singing from their lair,
The flowers revive, and look, as ever, fair;
The evening shade speaks to us of the heat
Absorbed and given back in beads complete

Of dew ; to-morrow's sun will lift
The wealth of vapour—such is solar thrift.
The tender blades and cups of flowers rejoice
E'en in this process, largely have a voice.

And still the show holds on ; now chafers swarm,
And hosts of midges banquet in the warm
And life-inspiring rays.   Finches and tits
Go gathering food all day while light permits ;
Within the tangled hedge the prickly brere
Protects the redbreast who is building there ;
Ferns in the warren now in luxury wave,
And help to hide what seems a rabbit's grave ;
From morn till eve you'll see these gamesters skip
And gambol, spite of thunder, cloud, and drip ;
The yellow-hammer on the hedge you'll spy,
And wagtail on the road, as you pass by,
In song persistent or in pool at play :
And thus is passed a lengthy Summer's day !

To each of Nature's children do we owe
A trace of joy as on in life we go ;
Be it a song, a scent, glimpse of delight,
Each helps to make our earthly sojourn bright ;
Each takes a hallowed place in Nature's dance,
And of her love towards us shows a glance,
Glads us with morning kisses.   Welcome, June !
Who cannot to thy joys his heart attune ?
Who fain to thy fair days would say farewell,
Or tire upon thy glories e'er to dwell ?
Then let us love thee long and use thee well.

Ballades.

I.

ON LIFE AND HOME.

How dark a picture when we're young
  Appears this life ! What feeble glow
Lights up the canvas ! Every rung
  Of hope's long ladder seems a foe
  To mounting upwards. Long ago
The dirge was sung : "Oh, what a fight
  Minerva's flowers it is to blow !"
Home is the keynote of delight !

Effort and struggle—heart and lung
  With boyhood's fire soon bend the bow
That slays despair, and hopes new strung
  Lift us on fuller waves that flow.
  The storms that rage, the winds that blow,
We breast with growing manly pride ;
  Our cruise winds up with "Tally-ho !"
Home is the keynote of delight !

New scenes, new faces, oft among,
   In life's career we wandering go
To cities famous, lands oft sung,
   In quest of health or wealth, and grow
   Weary at vanity's poor show;
And still uncloyed's our appetite,
   Of joy we find no overflow—
Home is the keynote of delight!

REFRAIN.

Cymbals may echo, bugles blow,
   Pæans of pilgrims exquisite;
But I'll be no Bohemian Joe—
   Home is the keynote of delight!

II.

THE CRY OF A BROKEN HEART.

ERE half her bloom of beauty had been blown,
  And woman's ripeness she had scarcely seen,
The Phyllis of my muse had felt the frown
  Of crimson-fingered Fate, that ruthless queen,
Whose subtle step e'en taints the best renown.
No cup of pleasure's left, all mirth has flown,
  Weird forms of anguish haunt her bosom keen,
Life's now reduced to an unconscious moan,
  No forecast of the storm has fortune's chart
Marked out for her.   We hear from seeds once sown
  Only the cry of a broken heart !

Ere destiny had marked her for its own
  She was the fay of mirth, and joy terrene;
In halcyon days of youth she wore the crown,
  The glittering ring of hope, and stood, I ween,
A watchword unto men, of mind serene.
No longer does her smile sunshine impart,
  Despair alone depicts her abject mien—
Only the cry of a broken heart !

The victim of remorse, no longer known,
    Speechless in wrinkled grief and quite unclean
She wretched stands, of woe the corner-stone,
    Delusion's princess, misery's machine !
Urge her and comfort her, and nought you'll glean,
    Save that " she's lost," in heaven will take no part :
A vale of tears alone is hers, I ween—
    Only the cry of a broken heart !

Refrain.

Though cycles of health and " all's well " are oft shown,
    Few homes are unscathed by delusion's fell dart ;
To dear ones left behind how oft murmurs the moan—
    Only the cry of a broken heart !

III.

ON OLD LOVES.

To think of the past how we all feel delight !
 How we love to reflect on the goblet of joy
We quenched at love's torch ! Who wouldn't indite
 The ardour his heart entertained when a boy—
 How his pulses kept tune to the sweets of the coy !
Although our bark's trimmed and our ensign says, Nay,
 Get along; with the shallows of life do not toy !
Farewell to the loves of a youth's heyday !

But the apple forbidden I'd still wish to bite,
 A moment with Annie I thirst to enjoy,
Though friendly alone would be vows now to plight,
 Were I equally smitten—I now couldn't buoy
 Her hopes as of yore, and her fate would destroy
Any prospect of mine o'er her heart having sway :
 So with Elsie ; I'd have to rejoin, damsel coy—
Farewell to the loves of a youth's heyday !

But time is a healer, heartrendings despite,
 Or moments on Pattie I now would employ,
How she dreamt of me always as gallantest knight,
 And thought I alone could her fond wishes cloy.

Howe'er too, again, I came to destroy
Those ties too with Nora I never can say.
How the beaux of the girls must the mothers annoy !
Farewell to the loves of a youth's heyday !

Refrain.

O'er the calm sea of bliss—my dream when a boy !—
  That I tranquilly sail, I've only to say,
May wedlock's trim ferry my "fancies" convoy ;
  Farewell to the loves of a youth's heyday !

THE MERRY HUM OF INSECTS IN THE AIR.

I.

When the swallows dive and dart,
   And the little birds take heart,
In the gala month of June, when all is fair,
   When sunshine decks the hedges,
   And true to all their pledges
Keep the feathered pets of song that love its glare,
   I know nought so composing,
   To lullaby disposing,
Like the merry hum of insects in the air.

II.

When peasants are haymaking,
   And the gentle breeze is shaking
All the virgin blades of bearded wheat and tare,
   While the larks their young are feeding,
   And the busy bees are speeding
To their hives, and cells are building layer on layer,
   I know no flight or flutter,
   Not the tit's trip can I utter,
Like the merry hum of insects in the air.

N

III.

When the haytime's fairly over,
　And we picnic on the clover,
And for canopy the sky alone have bare,
　How pleasant 'tis to ramble
　On the bracken, watch the gambol,
See the hurry, skurry, hurry of the hare !
　But pleasanter to listen
　'Tis to life that's just uprisen,
Like the merry hum of insects in the air.

IV.

To hear the throstle's treble
　We take a lot of trouble,
To the hazel-coppice cheerily repair ;
　When tired of human chatter
　We love to hear the patter,
Of the rainfall's patter-patter have a care,
　But no music makes us doze,
　Ever tempts our eyes to close,
Like the merry hum of insects in the air.

V.

When rowing down the river
　How we love to hear the quiver
Of the breeze-tost weeping-willow branches spare,
　See the waters plunge in torrents
　At the weir ! though in abhorrence

Are its foam and roar by maids held everywhere ;
　Though linnets' notes are merry,
　No murmur's at the ferry
Like the merry hum of insects in the air.

VI.

　When touring in the tropics
　As a pilgrim of all topics,
Perhaps the hissing of the snake makes greatest scare ;
　The ringing of the cymbals,
　Tom-toms, or Afric' tymbals
May in discord next most certainly compare ;
　But no hum e'er makes us ponder
　On the prairie, thrills with wonder,
Like the merry hum of insects in the air.

A SUMMER SERMON.

I.

ATOMS of Summer waft across the mead
  In waves of ether, pollen-laden warm ;
    Bees, butterflies now feed
  Upon the honey'd cups, plenteous in swarm
And merry hum, and he who runs may read
  The gala chronicle of glee, his goblet steep
  In Nature's mine of plenty birthday keep
At Flora's banquet ; now July is here,
So largely drink its sunbeams, court its cheer !

II.

Put on thy festive tints, ye favoured fair,
  And gather in the wavelets that abound
    Of renovating air !
  List to the symphony of birds, the sound
Of music from the tangled thicket where
  The linnet pipes, the nightingale wells out
  His evensong of joy to ears devout :
No longer be a chrysalis ; thy home
Of stinted rays oft quit, seek heaven's dome.

III.

Hie to the woodland, stream, or moor of gorse
　　While thy limbs feel the pulse of youth, the glow
　　　　Of animated force,
　　And harvest gather to an overflow
Of strength!　Alacrity brings no remorse,
　　Pleasure or profit bound; awake from sleep
　　At Summer's pageant.　Feel each peep
Of solar glory.　Fleeting clouds may seem
To linger, but soon comes Aurora's beam.

IV.

Like to the rose, the leaf of life's soon here
　　That shows the russet tint, the bloom's decayed
　　　　That lent a glory to the year;
Even so do youth and beauty early fade:
Then linger on the lulling sounds that cheer
　　The peasant's daily toil :—the blackbird's scream,
　　The singing corn, the purling of the stream,
The soothing songs that echo from the trees
In tides of melody that much appease!

V.

Go to the fields to view the carnival
　　Of winged and feathered tribe, to watch the glee
　　　　Of life, both great and small:
The pheasant's flap, ant's tour, dexterity
Of lynx-eyed squirrel, gold-fly, festal squall

Of fledgling peeping o'er the brim of nest :
Then listen to the song of loved redbreast,
To know that Summer moves, and that her bank
Of beams is ours, no matter what our rank !

VI.

Let not your eyes grow dim for want of use
　　In forward-seeing ; never backward turn
　　Your mental gaze ; the rather choose
To follow out life's programme to the stern
And final note of conscience, ne'er to lose
　　The crown of industry !　Weep by the brook
　　Rather than whine at tasks in your set nook ;
Men's minds grow larger when no more confined
To selfish issues—wiser, more refined.

VII.

Our happiness depends on what we do,
　　Not for ourselves, but others.　To the hive
　　　　Of social weal is due
Each toiler's honey.　Every one must strive
　　To feed the skep, or else his life he'll rue
In senile winter.　Like the busy bee,
　　Then hum all day in glee ;
Let each gay summer-time your courage wake,
And doughty deeds you'll surely undertake.

ON THE BEACH.

I.

OFF for a holiday, duty being done,
  Set off to Yarmouth Beach,
  Features to freckle and bleach,
Ye searchers of health ! for the sea and the sun
  Afford the richest gem,
  Brightened with negro-fun :
There Aurora brings joy, zephyrs each,
  And raptures marine who would stem
  E'en for a hermit's diadem ?
    Sing on, then, minstrel boy !
    Life's chill needs some alloy ;
    Be festive, and zephyrs enjoy
      On the Beach !

II.

Plunge in the sea, every one ;
  Taste of the salt sea-cup
Before you on shingle do run.
Don't be in pluck e'er undone ;
Catch the ozone in a boat,
Each other's pleasure promote,

Till you get bloom of peach
   From the surf and the spray
   On your glad holiday
    On the Beach !

III.

Don't be too sordid, clinging to pelf ;
   A time set aside to rejoice,
Our vigour's soon laid on the shelf—
   Such is the wise traveller's voice.
Let us all have a care for our sowing
   Our seed ere our noonday's spent,
Ere Nature's fell blast comes a-blowing,
   And youth's lusty frame is too bent
To repair to the shore of The Broads,
Right away from the counting-house frauds,
   Where I've heard that no calm
    Doth the citizen reach,
   Like the health-scented balm
    On the Beach !

IV.

A whiff of ozone at sea,
   Wrack-tainted is the breeze I love ;
Nought of the land-gale for me,
   Though I to Gorleston ville rove.
None of your crack-jolly "sails" outward bound,
   But a yacht trimmed for my craft
That will creek navigate when "all's found,"
   And yield sport afore and abaft !

On the lake, 'neath the cover, on sand—
Remember 'tis Peggoty's land—
   Then make for yon reach
Where the wherries lie snug on the strand,
   Holding close as a leech ;
See the crew making nets with the hand,
Ere their stores they tranship, crew disband,
      On the Beach !

v.

Agreed then, we go for a sail !
   See the waters of Breydon,
Also Oulton Broad we mustn't fail ;
All to get ruddy and hale,
   Not back to return till we've laid on
A day rich in tan, ere the jetty,
   We tacking, return in *The Maiden ;*
When our craft the natives we'll teach
   Sitting at rest on the settee,
Wild ducks and skates
We'll bring to our mates
      On the Beach !

vi.

Time presses.   We now sail and see
   Fritton, the queen of the lakes ;
   So pack up the pies and cakes,
From the shore's din let us both flee,
   Join the anglers and sketchers at work
    Hard by some shaded nook,

Watch the perch full of play—how they shirk
   A fisherman's eye, oft his hook :
Sail beside the decoy, hear the coo
Of the wild pigeon (what a to-do !)
   Ere we steer through the breach
And return to the briny and blue ;
   When our bags we'll preach
To the home-folk, our escapades too
On The Broads, when at sea, in a stew
   On the Beach !

THE DAWN OF DAY.

AN ODE.

WHO doesn't feel a perfect peace to reign,
  A virgin freshness when the morning star
  Heralds the light of day, holds sway afar
In twinkling solitude, above the plane
Of human vision? Who would deign
  To slumber on, nestled in bed of down,
  Who duly weighed the wealth a crimson crown
Of solar rays can shed in morn's campaign?
  No longer would be hushed in second sleep
The searcher after health, life's charioteer;
  No longer in oblivion would steep
The enthusiast life's goblet—he would steer
  On from the very dawn his fragile bark,
Losing no draught of health-inspiring stream,
          Light after dark,
          When trills the lark,
Can give to man in renovating beam!

Yet mankind wastes the fragrance of the morn,
  Though all is then attuned in our domain
To deeds of excellence, with children born
  To tread ambition's ladder, to attain
          Life's granary of corn!

Aurora's fertile beams flow on unknown,
　While youth and age wear still the coronet
Of slumbering Morpheus; while the pilfering drone
　Sips floral nectar from the violet,
Erewhile the throstle's recitative's poured
　Forth from the copse, and all the birds have sung,
Creation's lord has slumbered, and has snored
　On quite unconsciously, and ne'er upsprung.

Nought, save the browsing cattle, mars the peace
　Of yonder homestead, save a rabbit's skip,
　　　The cackle of the geese;
Or else the soothing rustle of the leaves
　Of stately poplar-trees, perchance the drip
Of rainfall from o'erhanging and thatched eaves:
　　　Then rise and bind the sheaves,
　And teach the world the feats of workmanship:
　　　　At early dawn
　　　No longer sleep and yawn,
　Contented you a fuller life have drawn.
The honeyed sweets may linger on the way,
But your alacrity will not gainsay
　Place with the throng of workers in the strife,
Or industry's reward another day,
　Whether you have bairns or but a wife,
So long as you betimes get in the hay.

True feats of husbandry begin at dawn;
　Plodders of hand and head then gain a march
O'er their compeers.　Sleek blackbirds on the lawn

Then make their matin-feasts, no longer parch
   The young of warrenkind ; the lime and larch
Attest the rival loves then of winged tribe ;
   All Nature pulsates to the magic wand
Of life-evolving sunshine ; bees imbibe
Now nectar from the cups, to hives subscribe
   In form of luscious honey ; leaves expand,
   Petals unclose, flowers beautify the land—
Chaste morn-saluting children of the sun !
   Then *carpe diem*, wanderer ; don't be dead
To rosy morn's health-tempered rays, my son ;
   Unloose the bonds that lash you to your bed.

THE QUEEN OF NIGHT.

ODES.

I.

Thou lesser lamp, that hoverest like a spell
  Around our globe fecund! thou Queen of Night,
  Mirror of solar bounty, borrowed light,
We pay thee homage, to thy altar tell
  Our beads of obligation, for thy boon
    To us poor denizens when past the gloaming;
Twilight has gone, and handed thee, O Moon,
    The reins of government, the shadowing
Of his resplendent beams! Thy face,
Though many-figured, glads our race
  When oft pursuing voyage wholly
    Lost in direction, on tempestuous deeps,
  And on so-called "earth-time" depending solely.

Through thee the mariner position reaps
 By thy fixed fleeting tour within the sky,
Eastward or westward; of all fleeting cars
 Thou art a ruling index, accurately
Place—by thy moving sphere among the stars—
 Is told to men, thy glorious robe
Above the deep points out the shoals and bars
 To wandering pilgrims on a restless globe.

II.

Thou art the fairy queen of harvest-tide
 When in full glory, for thy flood of light
 Assists to garner to the topmost height
The mellowed fruits of earth both far and wide.
 Such is thy glad illumination,
  Thy services of bounty never cease,
 No matter what thy face, thy station.
  The monarchs of the deep thou canst release
 By force of tidal flow, by power
 Magnetic on the waves. Thy dower
To ocean's lift to fuller heights of flow,
 Is equally as bounteous, thy mass
To influence the submerged earth below.
 That wealth of waters nothing can surpass;
And still thy virtues speak aloud, O Queen!
  Seasons and festivals by thee are set;
That which is known as " Paschal" thy serene
 Bright face decides, as though the fullest light
 Alone became the risen Saviour's flight;
  As though the tragedy that paid the debt
 Of human ill invoked the Queen of Night!

III.

Like to the torch of day's thy silvery face
    Circling 'mid thousand lesser lights above,
    Had equal meed of governing when Jove
Of old the fates decreed of human race ;
Thy mystic motion 'twas set shepherds wandering,
   Chaldean of old, away from sleeping herds ;
And Eastern races still—during their praying—
   Deem thee oracular in fate ; no words
Can paint thy pagan powers, no pen
Portray what once thou wert to men !
   But such is mythic, Dian ; for thy beaming
With fuller history and fuller life
   Is now so full of ken !   No dreaming
Omens about thee now awaken strife,
    Though thou dost still obtrude thy darkened frame
      Across glad Phœbus' path, though thou dost tour
    Around his might in rhythm just the same
As thou wert wont of old within the skies.
We know thy purpose, grandeur, mass, and size,
     'Though dark dew-laden clouds as oft obscure
In northern climes thy face, thy smiles disguise.

IV.

Who hasn't sought thy company at eve,
   When heart-beats tuned to love have raged in youth
   And madly surged for echo?   Who, in truth,
Would fain deny thee at the taking leave
   Of his ideal?   'Thou art a witness cherished,

No matter what the season, of love's troth.
  Who dallying 'neath thy gleams hath not nigh perished,
Though his heart's been afire at taking oath
    Of fond allegiance? We court thy gracious reign,
    Thou art the beacon of fair love's campaign ;
Thy mellow glow awakes the nightingale
    To sweetest song, stirs to his toil the bat,
Is welcome to the owl, when evening veil
    Crowns hill and moor. And who can look up at
Thy pristine brightness, not inquire the whence
    Thine origin and what thy meaning there?
Does thy bright face glad other countenance
    Than this fair orb's? Do planes to men unknown
    Feed on thy radiance, bask beneath thy throne?
Who of thy riches would deny a share?
    Who would a portion of thy beams disown?

v.

Thou art the peerless goddess of the vast
    Terrestrial sea of space ! Thou dost preside
    O'er regions past our ken and hope beside.
Leases of life are thine, for ere thy last
    Circuit of splendour's o'er, thy locks so waving
To us-wards an aureola declare—
    (For glimpses of Aurora we've a craving !)
We see a light crescentic deck thy hair,
    Thy fuller charms greet other space,
    Until we catch thy glad " half-face."
Where dost thou sojourn, goddess? Whence thy circling
    Thus as Earth's mate, and thus to spend thy days,

o

" At sea," in foreign realms commingling,
    Spending thy capital in unknown ways?
But what a queen thou art when solar wealth
    Lights up thy face " at full " !   Thou art the prize,
Creation's medal, that dispenses health,
    Spite of thy light being elsewhere spent again,
    Thy smiles directed to another plane,
When quite three-quarters " gone " within the skies,
    Yet thou the Queen of Night dost still remain !

ON SIMULATING YOUTH.

(A SATIRE.)

INTO the market-place, the gay saloon
Whither the lions hie, the minstrel-boy,
The little critic (elfin, if you like)
Escorts you smiling, bent on pointing out
The mockery, the sham pretence of those
Who by the tricks of art, the props of skill
Cosmetic, " of the mode," affect to cheat
Us all by putting back the clock of age.
  Behold within the Fair of Vanity
The peacock-damsel decked to imitate
The finished and becurled wax caste of art
In beauty, architecture—all for youth
Or youthful semblance !   Yet to put off time
Would seem to shadow forth a fear of death,
Although the prayer upriseth constantly,
" That life a mourning is, that rest is sweet."
There is the man of means within the mart,
Who, too, hides his grey locks from the rude gaze,
Smooths out the growing furrow of time's march ;
He, too, puts back the enemy a span,
Tries to affect a lie !—being sixty quite,

He longs to pose as forty, cheat the mass ;
Yet all the while he tells you he believes
In immortality, spite of his arts,
Manœuvres to the wicked contrary ;
The game he plays for's credit, affluence
In years uncounted of prosperity.
You laughingly pass on.   Another scene—
Along the Row—helps you to get behind
The worn-out roué's pencilled brows of care.
Alas ! too often prompted by days spent
In reckless folly ; read between the lines
The ravages of time, the sicklied mien,
That haggardness—the child of stern remorse !
He reigns at large, pinched in the waist by art,
Bereft of ruddy youth, yet foolishly
Affecting youth in collar built erect
And carrying a crook—the modern prop
Of " masherdom."   In cuff of overstarched
And needless length, he, too, the artifice
Of costume imitates, to trick the eye
And mask the march of time by such device
As ingenuity suggests in gewgaw, fob,
Cosmetic artifices, of which *rouge*
And *noir*, with wigs becurled, are not unknown.
But we must wend our steps another way.
Yon lady " well preserved " (?) attracts your gaze,
Deceives you in her youthful charms, her face
Beneath the glitter of the gay saloon ;
(Though beauty unadorned, she grants, is grace).
And what a task !   With what a toil she decks
Those features that alone proclaim her soul !

With what a care she crimps, she freshens up
Her borrowed ringlets, tries to efface the lines
Left by the sands of time, ere the last act,
"The touch of triumph," comes ; no studio
For properties of pigment, brushes, balms,
Like to her greenroom surely can compare.
Her cells of ivory and coral too
Tell the same tale—this handicapping time !
How wicked, how deceitful is it all—
This trade in unguents, tinsel, and red tape,
Fallals of falsity, fair fashion's "trumps" !
And still the shuttle flies, the farce is spun :
Yet how it fails so often to deceive !
What a detective is the light of day
To all this trickery !   You need but go
And view the actor's back to see the sham—
Burlesque on time—performed the other side,
Divine the hieroglyphics printed there.
I've seen them often.   Nature never lies !
The ridges left by yesterday's full tide
Can't be effaced, not even by the flood
Of buoyant humour and assumed content
That's hidden beneath a coat of "Gilead's balm."
Wrinkles alone but typify retreat
Of vital welfare, are but a receipt
For time that's past, for pulses that have moved
The organs of expression in full play ;
They are the lines that cancel out the days
That have been seen, that are beyond recall.

JOTTINGS ON A SCOTCH TOUR.

I.

VERY shortly we shall meet
Northern air to breathe, so sweet;
For arrivéd has the time
When we seek a change of clime.
Though my heart remains at home,
Timely tempted, I must roam,
Get away from toil and care,
Enemies to our welfare.

II.

Swiftly on a Northern line
Am I carried then, in fine;
Land o' Cakes, King Arthur's Seat,
Will I rightly, gladly greet.
Doubting nought too, I decide
To steamer take adown the Clyde,
Whose azure stream has no compeer
For island, ben, or loch or weir.

III.

Isles of romance long ago,
Fascinating fancy now,
Deck its waters free from foam,
Tranquil till you seawards roam ;
Promontories, creeks, and bays
On each bank arrest your gaze ;
Perched upon the river's bank
Now's a laird's home (man of rank !) ;
Clustered green groves there abound
As we smartly steam around ;
On the deck now trills the lute,
Soon we're in the Kyles of Bute.

IV.

Who for beauty can gainsay
Picturesqueness of Rothsay ?
On its pier wait pa and ma,
There you'll see the gondola.
Breeze attuned to Northern sky
But dismisses Italy.
Health and order mark the town,
Venice-like, that courts renown ;
Floating craft of every sort
Typify this favoured port ;
Thrifty Scot there waits 'longside,
In your tour to act as guide.

v.

Engine's pant and pace define
Rugged coast of Bannatyne;
Heath-clad mountains now uprise,
Oft snow-crownéd, to the skies.
For Loch Riddon now we make,
Frith that's like a land-locked lake;
Note the course now steamer steers
Spite of march from "Gondoliers;"
Senses quite enthralled for miles
Quite beguile us through the Kyles.

vi.

Oft you think you're on the Rhine—
Now you know you're on Loch Fyne;
Wealth of waters, mighty span,
Soon will brace us up with tan,
Zephyrs laden with ozone
Quickly gird with weal of tone;
Bruce's land and Tarbert Pier
Shortly into view come near.
Stopping, we take matin feast
Ere she steams ahead nor'-east;
Ere we see the land of briers—
Ardrishaig—our system tires.

VII.

Disembark, and re-embark
On *The Linnet* ere it's dark.
Now we're in Crinan Canal;
Tinkle, tinkle goes the bell.
Honeysuckle, eglantine,
Bluebell, heather, and woodbine
Grow on banks by nature sown;
Falling water—purest known—
Now descends in rippling shock,
Filtered through a granite rock.
Rising lochs delay our course,
Tempt us to the hill of gorse;
Falling lochs of waters black
Equally make wheel run slack:
Glow of sunshine, ether blue,
Pace withal, ne'er weary you;
Beech of bronze and peasant belle
Greet you as you quit canal.

VIII.

Jura's sound now opens out
Panorama grand *en route*—
Mountains, islets, snuggest bays,
Basking in glad Phœbus' rays.
Now we're in the land of Lorne,
Dear to sons of Argyle born.
Granite boulders, rocks of slate,
Tumbled, quarried, point to fate;
Blasts volcanic in past time
Here have blown—effect sublime!

X.

Corryvrecken's gulf's now seen
Like a whirlpool, isles between—
That of Scarba, Luing's shore!
Watch the gulls there wildly soar—
Halt, refresh at Black Mill Bay—
Scottish home of Collinsay—
Till the steamer's paddles pull
Full in sight of mighty Mull;
Ere Kerrera's straits you span
Reach your trysting-place—Oban!

XI.

Rail and paddle, coach, there ply,
Round about right merrily;
Highlands rich in loch and glen,
Winding lake and mammoth ben
There abound from west to east,
Yielding each of sight a feast.
Modern villes there dotted rise
On the slopes of mounds of size;
Yachts becalmed rest in the bay,
Trimming sails for service gay;
Ruined castles, ivy-bound,
Meet your eye in merry round.

Fir plantations yonder loom,
Verdant to the crack of doom ;
Jolly-boats, a motley crew,
There await to welcome you ;
Scions loyal of ancient clans
Ready e'er to meet your plans,
Take you to Iona's shore,
Glencoe's Pass, or furthermore
Festive make you as you go
With their cheery "Tally-ho !"

CHRISTMAS CHIMES.

I.

LISTEN to the Christmas waits!
Note the story song relates
  Of the birth of One in stall,
  Who glad tidings brought to all!
Nazareth no home is able
  Him to give at coming; careless,
  Cold is Jewish heart at sadness,
Pangs of hallowed maid in stable.

    Herod Great in Galilee
    Revelled at Nativity;
      In a grotto was Christ born
      King of men, though comfort shorn.
    Think of this at Christmas glee!

II.

Listen to the minstrel voice
Warbling plaintively, " Rejoice,
  Peace, goodwill towards men," is come!
  Listen to the chorus, drum!

Angels hovered, heavens rended,
   Kings brocaded came to ponder,
   Wise men from the East to wonder,
Star of splendour birth attended.

     May thy Christmas morning dawn,
     Though the snow be on the lawn,
       Free from chill or care at home !
       Never let thy gladness roam
     Till the Yule-tide log's withdrawn !

III.

Listen to the carillon
Echoing peel in belfry yon !
   Jubilee of joy is rolled,
   Out the " old, old story's " told.
The village church is decked with taste,
   Choice figures picked in lily-white,
   Red-berried emblems greet the sight
With wreaths of ivy, moss—so chaste !

     Listen to the anthem there !
     Of your riches something spare
       Halt and hungry !   Be at peace
       With mankind, all discord cease !
     Then rejoice in Christmas fare !

Christmas 1889.

THE VIRGINIAN CREEPER

(AMPELOPSIS HEDERACEA).

WHO has not paused and banquetted in mind
    Upon the grace and luxury of growth
Shown by the creeper, whose lithe tendrils bind
    With robes of emerald our homestead, clothe
Our naked walls with beauty?   Who can find
    A clinger that possesses half the troth
Shown by the plantlet of Virginian fame?
Its very presence gives a tone, a name
    To the environs of our dwelling-place;
        Its wealth of foliage changes to a bower
        The portals of our home!   Such is its power
    To climb our walls, enveil them as with lace.
Its leaflets help to deck both damsel, dame
    When in autumnal glory, and its hues
In wild October are a household name
    As they adorn our fairy window views.

And yet it boasts not blooms or evergreen,
Is leafless, dreary too in winter seen,
    Spite of its richness at late summer's eve,—
Tassels of crimson, russet, amber, brown,
    Which represent the most bewitching wreath
Of the fair creeper in its reign e'er known.

How it adorns the decorative ware,
 Fruit laden, at the feast! Arcadia's bowers
  And tints of splendour surely can't become
More tastefully, such claim to notice share
 At festive hostess' board when summer flowers
  Are gone—more tastefully then glad the home.
Its powers of adaptation, too, engage
 A meed of notice. How its tendrils climb
 Thus aimlessly along stage after stage ·
Unto the highest point—the eaves sublime
 Decide its progress! Just as though a flash
  Went to the root to regulate the sap,
  The creeper halts in growth and takes a nap,
 Feeling that farther progress would be rash.
How the curved tendrils swell, become bright red,
And little discs develop, which too shed
 A juicy liquid that makes it adhere— ·
With strength sufficient to resist the gale—
 To the rude surface o'er which they career!
Even solar heat is now of no avail
Their grip to undermine, nor rain, nor hail.
How lavishly has Nature thus endowed
 This creeper thus to need nor culture, care,
Direction in its growing! We are proud
 To think this plant is common to our shores
 And beautifies the lintels of our doors.
It points a lesson to us : " Don't aspire
Beyond your reach, 'tis foolish to aim higher."
 "Self-help" e'er finds resources of its own,
  And oft attains, too, proud ambition's throne.

THE LEGEND OF ST. DOROTHEA.

(A PARAPHRASE.)

PAUSE at the threshold of this saddest theme ;
Unloose your sandals, ye who would the shrine
Of this fair saint pay homage at, who died
Purely for conscience' sake, and what her heart
Believed as truth.   'Twas in the ancient plain
My story opes, of Cappadocian fame,
That one named Dorothea lived, who gave
Her life blood for the cause, the hallowed light
Of Christian servitude, by prayers, by alms,
Fasting, and sacrifice.

                Of beauteous mould
And sweetest grace, there nowhere could be found
One like unto her in Samaria's land
Or humble tenement in Ephraim's vale ;
No beauty like to hers had such repute
On Cæsarea's coast ; no peasant's brow
Shone out in such nobility ; no orb
Of iris-tinted richness filled the soul
With adoration's raptures like to hers.
And yet her life was simple, serving God
With cheerfulness, alone at latest eve

Taking its rest; nought cared she for herself,
Hers was a life of purest sacrifice.
No rich man's slave cared she to be,
Or hireling at the market, at the port;
She loved the sick to tend, the poor to help,
Give comfort to the dying.   Now, there ruled
Within the province mentioned heretofore,
The Cæsarean city, one, by name,
Fabricius, who was Governor, whose stern
Imperious rule was hardened by his creed.
He was a pagan chief, whose unbelief
Had made him persecute the Christian sect;
And hearing of the spotless virgin maid—
Her widespread beauty and her signal charm—
He bade his officer before him bring
This Dorothea, fairest in the land.
With mantle folded round her surging breast,
And orbs devoutly, meekly, looking down,
The beauteous maid of sorrow entered in
The palace of the tyrant, and stood still.
Uncouth of speech, the Governor then said:
"Who art thou?" and she answered, "I am one
Named Dorothea, servant of the Lord
And follower of Christ, a virgin pure."
Then he, harshly, to this simple statement said:
"Thou must surely, damsel, serve our gods or die!"
When she further answered, mildly still cast down,
"Be it so, my lord!   The sooner I shall stand
Before the face of Him whom to behold
Is my fondest and most cherished of desires!"
Then the tyrant further questioned her, and said:

P

"Whom meanest thou, fair daughter?"   She replied:
"I mean the Son of God—Christ, mine espoused,
Who dwells in Paradise, and by whose side
Are everlasting joys, and in whose realm
Of starry splendour grow celestial fruits,
Roses that never fade or cease to charm."
Hereupon Fabricius, angry, overcome
By her modelled grace and by her eloquence,
Commanded her to prison to be led,
From which she'd just before but sallied forth;
And with passions raging, insolent and strong,
And a mind alone fermenting to despoil
Her unsullied scrip of virtue, he essayed
To make a convert of this Christian maid,
Ere numbering her among his fallen slaves.
With purpose such, two messengers he sent—
Calista and Christeta—who had once
The faith observed which Dorothea held,
But who from terror now had quite renounced
Their purer lives.   And promised rewards,
These sisters now tripped forth but to induce
The unhappy maiden to forswear her faith,
And fall a prey to this stern tyrant's will,
Rather than suffer death.   But, full of hope,
Courage, and constancy, the imprisoned girl
Reproved them strongly, and spoke out as one
Having authority: she further drew
In eloquence a picture of the joys
Her erring sisters each had given up
Through cowardice and falsehood.

Then they fell
At her feet, crying: "Oh, thou blessed saint,
Pray for us, Dorothea, that through thee
Our sins may be forgiven, and at the throne
Of grace our penitence accepted be."
And this she did. And when they both returned
Before the tyrant, robed in gaudy state,
They cried aloud: "We're servants of the Lord!"
Quite enraged, the Governor now swore and raved,
Commanding the two converts to come forth;
And he promptly sentenced each one to the flames:
But to Dorothea his decree relaxed,
For he sentenced her alone to watch the fire
That kindled flames of vengeance round the slaves.
And standing by, the faithful girl looked on,
Encouraging them bravely to endure,
And she cried aloud: "Oh, suffer to the end,
My sisters; fear not, for these transient pangs
Shall be followed by the joys of fullest life."
Thus they died! And Dorothea was condemned
To be tortured, put in chains, and then to die
By Fabricius, lord of tyranny and crime.
Nothing fearing, she endured with fortitude
The first portion of the barbarous sentence named,
Then cruelly was marshalled forth to die.
And as she went along, there passed that way
A young lawyer, who was named Theophilus,
Who had been a witness of her sentence dire;
And he called to her thus mockingly and said:
"Ah, maiden fair! and whither goest thou?
Is't to join thy favoured bridegroom up above?

I pray thee, send me down the fruits and flowers
Of that garden thou so eloquently spake,
For I would also taste of them, enjoy."
And Dorothea, with her head inclined,
Then looked on him, and with a gentle smile,
Said: "Thy request, Theophilus, I grant."
Whereupon he laughed aloud and sallied forth
With his heathen friends, but she went on—to die.
The stake was fully ready, but the cross
Was absent, the rich offering to redeem;
And Dorothea then knelt down and prayed;
And suddenly appeared at her side
A boy of beauteous mien, and radiant locks
That sunbeams flashed, "a smooth-faced glorious thing,
With thousand blessings dancing in his eyes."
He held a fairy basket which contained
Fresh-gathered apples, fragrant roses too;
And to the angel, ere she rose, she said:
"These, brother, carry to Theophilus,
Saying, Dorothea solely sends them him,
And that she goes before him to the place
Whence these offerings came—that she awaits him there;"
And with these words she sought the stake and died.
Meanwhile the angel went to seek the man,
Theophilus by name, whom laughing still
In merry mood he found, though quite alone,
And he placed the fairy basket full of flowers
And fruits celestial there before him, saying:
"Dorothea sends thee these," and vanished.
Thereupon Theophilus was thunderstruck,
And his conscience smote him keenly, and his heart

Nigh melted for remorse at what he'd said ;
And he tasted of the fruit, life-giving, brought
Thus miraculously by this angel fair ;
And he entered on a new life, and forthwith
Proclaimed himself a servant of the Lord
Like unto Dorothea, full of grace :
And he suffered with her for the cause of truth,
Like constancy, and furthermore obtained
A heavenly prize—the crown of martyrdom ! [1]

[1] For a more detailed account of this sacred legend see *Fraser's Magazine*, 1849. 2 vols. London. By Mrs. Jameson.

Rondeaus and Rondelets,

ETC.

I.

"SWEET EGLANTINE."

Sweet Eglantine ! with what a grace
Thy rosy cups deck out the race
  Of hymeneal maids ! 'Twas Eve
  First o'er thy pallor deigned to breathe
The kiss of love, and blushed thy face :
No wonder, then, that damsels place
Thy blossoms on their bridal lace ;
  Thy purity's no make-believe,
    Sweet Eglantine !

Thy witchery in the East we trace,
For Persians prize thy petals, chase
  Each other for thy blooms, and weave
  Love-posies round each other's sleeve :
And wedlock's links thy florets brace,
    Sweet Eglantine !

TRIOLET.

No matter how retired and coy,
   We soon get pierced by Cupid's dart ;
A lifelong solo cannot cloy,
No matter how retired and coy
The hidden self—it needs alloy
   To warm the beatings of the heart.
No matter how retired and coy,
   We soon get pierced by Cupid's dart.

II.

ADOWN OUR ROAD.

ADOWN our road what riches rare!
What sylvan forms, too, glad the air!
  The monarch of the forest pays
  Court to his bride—the elm, the mays,
Both white and tufted red, are there;
In stately line the chestnuts wear
A virgin bloom, and lilacs bear
  Bunches of fragrance, sweet mauve sprays,
          Adown our road.

The blossom of the cherry fair
Tones down the beech-trees' bronze of care,
  While lime-blooms bask in solar rays
  Close to the lofty firs—the gaze
Is full of beauty everywhere,
          Adown our road.

RONDELET.

" DANCE once again ! "
My Mirrie dear, if you've a mind,
          Dance once again !
Trip to the lyre ; I'll not complain,
Waltzing's a pleasure too refined
To murmur at, and " love is blind."
          Dance once again !

III.

IN SUMMER-TIME.

In summer-time with what a thrill
Of zest we follow pleasure, fill
  Up fleeting hours! There's not a day
  We do not court the sunny ray,
Or sojourn to some pleasant hill
Where the lark sings, or where the shrill
Note of the blackbird, linnet's trill,
  Echo around, make all things gay
    In summer-time!

We haunt the silvery stream, the rill,
We ply the oar where all is still,
  Our hearts unburdening on the way
  To those who treasure all we say,
Forgetting aught of worldly ill,
    In summer-time!

RONDELET.

" IF I were you,"
I'd, Ernest, wed a girl with gold,
　　If I were you.
I know they're far between and few,
And so I'd pick one ere you're old,
Buxom and ebon, not too bold,
　　If I were you.

IV.

THE SHAH—NASR-ED-DEEN.

July 1889.

Nasr-ed-Deen, of Royal Persian fame,
What, in thus starring Albion, was thy aim?
  Why didst thou leave that Eden, Teheran,
    With suite and "Mascotte" lad—Aziz-Sultan?
Was't British pageant, feast, or troop, or dame,
Or gatling-gun, bejewelled Shah ! thou came
To carry notions home, reform or tame
  Rebel Parsee or pampered courtesan?
                    Nasr-ed-Deen !
Farewell, dark monarch of imperious name,
Splendour of Western institutes proclaim
  On thy return to land of Ispahan,
    Set forth the stamp of the true Englishman ;
Thy morals, arts, court, dynasty reclaim,
                    Nasr-ed-Deen !

Rondelet.

"Confound that bee!"
I feel its bite still in my cheek;
    Confound that bee!
'Twas all through meddling with its glee
I paid the price I seemed to seek,—
A pang! which threats to last a week.
    Confound that bee!

V.

ACROSTICAL RONDEAU.

Hosts of good cheer are books to me,
Echoes of spirits gone to sea;
   Roam where I will, turn where I may,
   Be grave or gay, by night or day
Endless their power to cheerily
Revive life's way.   Minerva's tree
Tires less than social pleasantry;
   And that's why books remain, I say,
       Hosts of good cheer!

Snug draw the curtains; let me be,
My boon companions, then, with thee,
   Indoor beside the lamp's full ray:
   Theme—essay, epic, roundelay,
Heavy or light—you're all to me
       Hosts of good cheer!

RONDELET.

Down in my den,
Rich mental dainties rest in state
Down in my den.
Fiction and fact to feast the ken,
And poetry to elevate ;
Prized folios—all that men hold great,
Down in my den.

VI.

MY LITTLE GIRL.

My little girl I met at noon
At dawn of Spring; the waltz was done;
  Bright converse had we on the dance,
  The play, its votaries, fashion's prance,
Choice themes in fancy's garden strewn.
I found the song that would attune
Itself to her heart's strings, and soon
  Will echo words that will entrance
        My little girl!
I've met her oft in May and June
In floral alcove, with the moon
  Alone upon us—sweetest trance!
  She's told her love in looks askance,
And I've now found life's greatest boon,
        My little girl!

RONDELET:

Sequel to "Down in My Den."

"Look here or there!"
For prince of plays or chiefs of prose
    Look here or there!
A choir of songsters glads my lair—
Lodged with regard to rank in rows—
And wits abound to drown my woes;
    Look here or there!

VII.

SHE IS SO SWEET!

She is so sweet! I've never seen
In town or out so fair a queen;
  Her very smile glads my abode,
  Her every gesture's in my mode;
Her sweetness is as violets keen,
Fresh from a niche of grotto green;
So rich a voice, composed a mien,
  Her very graces claim an ode,
      She is so sweet!
Life was a lottery, I ween,
Before I found its hallowe'en;
  But I had travelled on the road
  Far into life, and felt its load,
Ere fate me led my pearl to glean—
      She is so sweet!

RONDELET.

"WHAT people say!"
I care not, doing this and that,
    What people say!
"For every dog must have his day,"
In spite of silly worldly chat
Of spies.   I do not care a sprat
    What people say!

VIII.

I LOVE HER SO !

I LOVE her so, she is my May
Queen, fitted for a roundelay !
   The sprite of freshness, oh, so sweet !
   I'll gently name her when we meet :
When clouds are dark she is a ray
Of light to cheer, a lamp alway,
At dew of eve, at dawn of day,
   In city, home, or country-seat—
     I love her so !

A boon companion at the play,
Where'er you go, where'er you stray,
   She is a perfect grace to greet,
   A lass to love, make joy complete
Throughout life's road till hair is grey—
     I love her so !

Rondelet.

" I'll go my gait ! "
E'en though I have to pay the toll,
        I'll go my gait !
No narrow code shall fix my fate,
Or baulk the path of freedom's soul
I cherish.   None shall me control ;
        I'll go my gait !

IX.

NEW YEAR'S EVE.

'Tis New Year's Eve! The Yule-tide log's ablaze,
And merry folks are home for holidays.
   Look yonder at the holly and the bay
    Circling the mantelpiece. There's rosemary,
And from the lintel mistletoe there sways;
The snow is on the ground, and lunar rays
Shine through the naked trees, yet youth essays
   To festive make the hearth with song and play—
       'Tis New Year's Eve!
The face of age e'en glows; peach-bloom arrays
The cheek of youth; bedecked in fashion's ways,
   Wedded and single dance to music gay;
    Peace and goodwill are watchwords from to-day,
Echoed by Father Time, who sings and says—
       'Tis New Year's Eve!

TRIOLET.

BRING out the bunting, deck the home,
 Make merry, for 'tis Christmas Day!
Feast as the folks all do at Rome,
Bring out the bunting, deck the home;
Toast all your friends in sparkling foam,
 Ye young and old, ye grave and gay!
Bring out the bunting, deck the home,
Make merry, for 'tis Christmas Day!

X.

BENEATH THAT FAN!

BENEATH that fan of gauze light pink,
Decked with white roses on the brink,
 With swallows painted on the frame
 Winging their way to heaven, came
Peeping from my coquette a wink
That fairly killed me—wicked blink!
Its very sauciness the chink
Assaulted, at my heart took aim
   Beneath that fan!

My chain of conquests gained a link
That eve in yon alcove.   I think
 The nymph's beyond the false flirt's fame;
 At all events she me o'ercame
Entirely 'neath it, made me shrink
   Beneath that fan!

Triolet.

Go and bask upon the beach,
  Far away from mental worry;
If your pallid face you'd bleach,
Go and bask upon the beach!
Doze while listening to the speech,
  Fun of minstrel boy, ne'er hurry;
Go and bask upon the beach,
  Far away from mental worry!

XI.

SUCH CHISELLED LIPS!

Such chiselled lips, such glossy ebon hair
  Fringing in clusters with a sylph-like grace,
A marble forehead has my Nina fair—
Sure evidence of intellect with care
  Tutored to young ambition, polished race.
Her face is rosy, round, and debonnair,
  Her dimples such as rondos fail to trace,
And ivory gates of speech, where play such rare,
      Such chiselled lips!

She plays the harp; we'd make a happy pair,
  For inspiration weds me to her face.
Celestial forms of beauty haunt the air
She breathes; none's like to her; my fondest prayer
  In this life's but to own this queen of grace,
      Such chiselled lips!

LIFE.

A TRIOLET.

THIS life's a play where health's the hero,
　　Fortune the fay we strive to court,
Spite of our chances being at zero.
This life's a play where health's the hero,
Lisping a cause : " Dum spiro, spero !"
　　How oft Fate chuckles at our sport !
This life's a play where health's the hero,
　　Fortune the fay we strive to court.

GET UP, GET UP, MY MERRY MAID!

RONDEL.

GET up, get up, my merry maid,
   The sun is arching high o'erhead,
The throstle's sung his serenade,
   Their matin-hymns the birds have said,
   Letters from home remain unread,
And hosts of duties need your aid.
Get up, get up, my merry maid,
   The sun is arching high o'erhead;

I know 'twas through that masquerade
   In which you flirted so with Ted
As " Flora."   What a queen you made?
   But surely now you're tired of bed !
Get up, get up, my merry maid,
   The sun is arching high o'erhead.

RONDELET.

"OF what he said,"
In whispers soft, I have no scent
    Of what he said.
I only know you turned so red
When to the grotto's shade you went;
But Ted's a flirt.   Not half is meant
    Of what he said.

254.

Hope.

> "Life now human would be brutish, just that Hope however scant
> Makes the actual life worth living, take the Hope therein away,
> All we have is surely not Endure another day:
> But the soul is not the body & the breath is not the flute,
> Both together make the music!" — Browning.

It is a child of Chance, a fickle fay
Betrothed to circumstance is Hope a sprite
That empties fancy's quiver & whose might
Dissolves the misery of Yesterday;

It is fortune's guide in pacing Life's highway
And buoys the warrior in the deadliest fight;
It writes on merit off with swallows' flight,
It is the planet of weird destiny.

'Twas medicine to the wretched Claudio's soul
And buoyed up Richard on a Bosworth field,
'Twas Milton's angel with the golden wings
Wedded to faith & Reason as a whole:
Though Gordon found in it a broken shield,
'Twas Stanley's anchor in his wanderings.

Aubrey de Smith

Dec 1906.

TRIOLET.

GRANTED my partner knows the game,
  I love to take a hand of whist;
His very lead suggests his aim,
Granted my partner knows the game;
His every tumble must proclaim
  What lingers in the other's fist.
Granted my partner knows the game,
  I love to take a hand of whist.

The Christmas Waits.
Rondo.

The Christmas Waits, wake up! they bring
Glad tidings on old time's fleet wing
  The "better land" sounds thro' the haze,
   Now, listen! there's a hymn of praise —
There's "Hark the herald angels sang!"
And Nazareth a Welcome ring!
   They are watchmen 'neath the pale
             moon rays,
The birth of Christ re-echoing —
        The Christmas waits.
On Cymbal, pipe & lute & string
As jack-a lanterns carolling,
  The burly knights of King Hal's days
   In gold & scarlet sang their lays
And to the olden ways we cling —
       The Christmas Waits.

Dec. 1906.   HAS.

Triolet.

He once was lionised by all,
   But Brown is quite an altered man;
He shone at dinner, rout, and ball,
He once was lionised by all,
A social prince with great and small;
I fear 'tis through an evil clan !
He once was lionised by all,
   But Brown is quite an altered man.

Roundels.

I.

WHEN I GO HENCE.

When I go hence to that cerulean sea
  Where reigns the Prince of Law, called Providence,
A conscious bird of flight I'd wish to be
            When I go hence,
Winging my way—the awed power knowing whence
  The universe acquires its harmony,
Will be to me an ample recompense :
Sight, organs suited to immensity
  I'd wish for, endless day and quickened sense,
To know the souls whose home's Eternity,
            When I go hence !

II.

BEAUTY, LOVE, TRUTH.

BEAUTY, Love, Truth—the watchwords of frail man—
　　I'd see made perfect, in perennial youth,
And mysteries solved that thinking cannot scan,—
　　　　Beauty, Love, Truth !

The reign of sin and evil, death uncouth,
　　Tempests and famines since the world began,
I'd see all conquered when I go, forsooth !

Realms of fresh wonders I'd delight to span
　　With souls of kindred ken, of rarest ruth :
With such I'd learn within the heavenly van—
　　　　Beauty, Love, Truth !

VILLANELLE.

PHYLLIS! is it nay, or wait?
  Since the dance you've hid your face,
Meet me at the churchyard gate!

I'm in a most love-lorn state,
  Like a knight who's in disgrace;
Phyllis! is it nay, or wait?

Time you've had to meditate,
  My fond vows I'll not retrace;
Meet me at the churchyard gate!

Cheerful hope in me's innate,
  Shall I win love's first embrace?
Phyllis! is it nay, or wait?

Five the hour, fifteenth the date—
  How I've missed your winsome face!
Meet me at the churchyard gate!

Get along, old Time, apace!
Mine is a most desperate case.
  Phyllis! is it nay, or wait?
    Meet me at the churchyard gate!

TRIOLET.

She's not "a blue," nor is she wise,
   But oh ! she's very loving, tender !
A merry twinkle glads her eyes,
She's not "a blue," nor is she wise ;
Her realm's her home, where she's a prize,
   Long may my lot be to defend her !
She's not "a blue," nor is she wise,
   But oh ! she's very loving, tender !

HUNTING SONG.

A VIRELAY.

I.

With the wind in the west,
And the scent at its best,
To the meet in good spirits I speed ;
I keep up with the rest
Of the fleetest contest
The claims of my thoroughbred steed ;
Bar and gate do I breast
In the chase as a guest,
Though the curs may the huntsmen mislead :
In a jacket of crimson I go, I go !
" Ya-ha-hoicks, tally-ho ! tally-ho !"

II.

O'er fence and o'er mead
No dangers I heed,
As my plunger's broad snaffle I guide ;
In the field do I lead
With the whip those indeed

Who on saddle themselves boast with pride;
    I ne'er halt for a feed
    With the hosts of good breed
Till reynard's to earth gone to hide:
  In a jacket of crimson I go, I go!
  "Ya-ha-hoicks, tally-ho! tally-ho!"

III.

    Well saddled I ride
    My charger astride,
With a pack of young hounds in full cry;
    Be the fence high or wide,
    I boldly decide
To dash through with credit, do I!
    With pluck on my side,
    I stem time and tide
To be hard on the hounds as they fly:
  In a jacket of crimson I go, I go!
  "Ya-ha-hoicks, tally-ho! tally-ho!"

IV.

    Though he prance, though he shy
    At his task, he must try,
Though he pant and he blow with his breath;
    O'er the moor he shall hie,
    Though to spurs he reply,
My proud steed shall be in at the death!
    At the yelp and the cry
    Of the hounds there hard by,
Will I list to my lord—"what he saith!"
  In a jacket of crimson I trow, I trow!
  "Ya-ha-hoicks, tally-ho! tally-ho!"

THE LANCERS.

A PANTOUM.

Pipe up, ye bandmen, away!
　Set in a figure of eight,
All ye that list in the fray,
　Each on his *vis-à-vis* wait.

Set in a figure of eight,
　Courtly advance and retire,
Each on his *vis-à-vis* wait,
　Daintily trip to the lyre.

Courtly advance and retire,
　Cross to the opposite side,
Daintily trip to the lyre,
　Lead home your lady with pride.

Cross to the opposite side,
　Half-way escorting her there,
Lead home your lady with pride,
　Swing in a romp to the air.

Half-way escorting her there,
  Keep well your time to a bar;
Swing in a romp to the air,
  Nought of the merriment mar.

Keep well your time to a bar,
  Ladies, all curtsey with grace;
Nought of the merriment mar
  When you the centre all face.

Ladies, all curtsey with grace,
  Pause till your knights join the ring,
When you the centre all face
  Each to "a fellowship" cling.

Pause till your knights join the ring,
  Gallop around in a chain,
Each to "a fellowship" cling
  Ere you get home once again.

Gallop around in a chain,
  Tour like a wheel round about,
Ere you get home once again,
  Rippling with laughter throughout.

Tour like a wheel round about,
  Visit the pair on the right;
Rippling with laughter throughout,
  Dapperly do the polite.

Visit the pair on the right,
  Left about wheel ! *chassez* there !
Dapperly do the polite,
  List to the lips of the fair.

Left-about wheel ! *chassez* there,
  Trippingly hie to your place,
List to the lips of the fair,
  Halt for "the chain" and "the chase."

Trippingly hie to your place,
  Gallop and *chassez* once more ;
Halt for "the chain" and its chase,
  After the grand march is o'er.

Gallop and *chassez* once more ;
  Be you the leader with care,
After the grand march is o'er,
  Ere to the lounge you repair.

Be you the leader with care,
  Yoke all the brave in a line ;
Ere to the lounge you repair,
  Greet, turn the fair and the fine.

Yoke all the brave in a line,
  Ere chimes the latest tra-la !
Greet, turn the fair and the fine,
  Ere leading home to mamma.

A FAREWELL SONG.

I AM tired,
Put out the light,
Shades of evening now are falling,
I must list to Nature calling
Me to slumbers, and go crawling :
I am tired, put out the light.
Fleet Pegasus, my wingèd steed,
The air is pawing me to lead.
Now 'tis night !
To fair realms where restful bliss
After toil comes not amiss.
I am tired, put out the light.
If I've pleased you, time will prove it,
All my aim has been to covet
Your ear for the muse—I love it
With my might.

Tingling are my ears this minute,
How I long to be its linnet !
I am tired,
Put out the light.

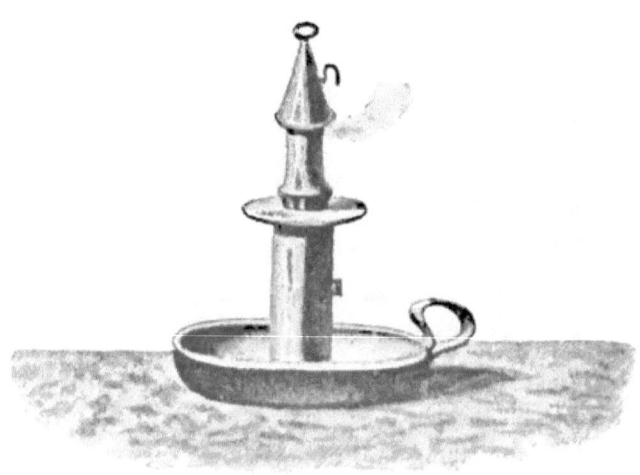

GOOD-NIGHT !

PRINTED BY BALLANTYNE, HANSON AND CO.
EDINBURGH AND LONDON.